Celebrate the Season

The
Twelve Pets
of
Christmas

The Twelve Pets of Christmas

by
Taylor Garland

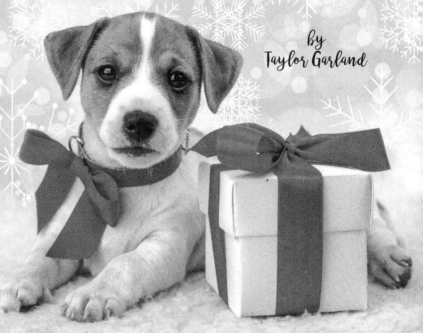

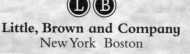

Little, Brown and Company
New York Boston

Copyright © 2017 by Hachette Book Group

Cover art © Smit/Shutterstock.com. Cover design by Christina Quintero. Photo credits: © Didecs/Shutterstock.com (ribbon), © Smit/Shutterstock.com (puppy), © digieye/Shutterstock.com (bow/frame). Cover copyright © 2017 by Hachette Book Group, Inc.

Hachette Book Group supports the right to free expression and the value of copyright. The purpose of copyright is to encourage writers and artists to produce the creative works that enrich our culture.

The scanning, uploading, and distribution of this book without permission is a theft of the author's intellectual property. If you would like permission to use material from the book (other than for review purposes), please contact permissions@hbgusa.com. Thank you for your support of the author's rights.

Little, Brown and Company

Hachette Book Group

1290 Avenue of the Americas, New York, NY 10104

Visit us at LBYR.com

First Edition: October 2017

Little, Brown and Company is a division of Hachette Book Group, Inc. The Little, Brown name and logo are trademarks of Hachette Book Group, Inc.

The publisher is not responsible for websites (or their content) that are not owned by the publisher.

Library of Congress Control Number: 2017939966

ISBNs: 978-0-316-47251-7 (hardcover), 978-0-316-47253-1 (pbk.), 978-0-316-47252-4 (ebook)

Printed in the United States of America

LSC-C

10 9 8 7 6 5 4 3 2 1

Chapter 1

Quinn Cooper didn't even want to blink. If she blinked, she might miss something—and there was so much to see! Finer Arts, the art supply store in Quinn's hometown of Marion, was her favorite place in the whole world.

Quinn trailed through each aisle—past the vibrant rainbow of paints; past the colored pencils in every hue imaginable; past handmade paper flecked with bits of gold and silver; past the long strands of glittering crystal beads. Every aisle inspired Quinn to start a new project. But now, she knew, was not the time. Not when she had so much to do!

Reluctantly, Quinn tore herself away from the handspun yarn section and headed toward the counter. The store's owner, Ms. Morimoto, smiled as Quinn approached.

"Hi, Quinn! I have a surprise for you," Ms. Morimoto began.

Quinn's eyes lit up. "Did they come? Did they come?" she asked.

"Voilà!" Ms. Morimoto announced as she pulled a red box from under the counter. Her eyes were twinkling as she passed it to Quinn. "Careful, now... they're very fragile."

Quinn held her breath as she eased off the lid. Nestled inside the box were twelve perfectly round ornaments, each one made of delicate blown glass. The ornaments reflected the bright lights overhead, but otherwise they were completely blank.

"They're perfect!" Quinn exclaimed. "Thank you, Ms. Morimoto!"

"It's my pleasure," the older woman replied. "I always try to make sure our special orders arrive as quickly as possible."

"The timing is *perfect*," Quinn said. "I'll be able to paint them over Thanksgiving break!"

"Are they for your family's Christmas tree?" asked Ms. Morimoto.

Quinn shook her head. "I'm going to donate them to the Marion Animal Shelter's fund-raiser," she replied. "They're kicking off a special event this year—the Twelve Pets of Christmas."

"Oh, yes—I've seen the flyers," Ms. Morimoto replied. "Tell me more."

"Mrs. Alvarez—she's the shelter director—well, she had this amazing idea," Quinn began. "The Twelve Pets of Christmas is a big promotional campaign to encourage people to adopt pets instead of buying them from a store. It kicks off with a fancy fund-raiser in ten days! There's going to be food, and dancing, and special Christmas cookies, and an auction with some really cool stuff, and portraits of the Twelve Pets that we especially hope will be adopted before Christmas. I'm donating twelve hand-painted ornaments. I'm going to paint animals on them."

"Genius!" Ms. Morimoto said. "I'm so impressed

that you're using your artistic talents for such a good cause, Quinn."

"It's the least I can do," Quinn said. "I love helping out at the animal shelter after school. And that's not all! At the benefit, I'll be—"

Quinn's voice trailed off.

"On second thought, maybe you could come see for yourself?" she continued. Quinn rummaged around in her backpack until she found a ticket to the fund-raiser. "All the volunteers got two free tickets. Would you like one of mine?"

Ms. Morimoto looked surprised, but only for a moment. Then a broad smile crossed her face. "I'd love to come. Thanks, Quinn!" she said as she took the ticket.

"Great! And that way you can see all the finished ornaments, too," Quinn replied. "I hope they turn out okay. I've never painted on glass before."

"I'm sure they'll be beautiful!" Ms. Morimoto assured her. "Just remember that the colors you use will shift a little, depending on the color of the ornament. And, you know, you could always add a little..."

Quinn waited expectantly while Ms. Morimoto reached under the counter again.

"Here you go—on the house." Ms. Morimoto gave Quinn a small jar of crystal glitter. "It's Christmas," she finished. "There's no such thing as too much sparkle!"

"Thank you!" Quinn said.

"Just sprinkle it on while the paint's still wet and you'll be good to go," Ms. Morimoto told her. "I'll see you at the benefit—and all your ornaments, too!"

"Bye, Ms. Morimoto," Quinn said as she carefully cradled the box of ornaments in her arms. "Thanks again—for everything!"

"Stay warm," Ms. Morimoto called out. "It looks like it's going to snow."

"I hope so!" Quinn said, laughing. "Bye!"

When Quinn stepped outside, she realized that it didn't just *look* like snow; it smelled like snow, too. That crisp, cold tang in the air was instantly recognizable. In her warm parka, Quinn didn't mind the chilly temperatures as she walked a couple of blocks home to the condo where she lived with her dad and their pet cat, Piper. It would be unusual to get a big snowstorm before Thanksgiving—but not impossible. Quinn couldn't help grinning as she remembered the massive blizzard that had hit Marion last winter, closing school for an entire week! Quinn and her best friend, Annabelle, had gone sledding on the big hill in Center Park for hours. Then, because school was closed, Annabelle got to sleep over at Quinn's house for two nights in a row!

It was a great memory—but it made Quinn a little sad, too. If there was a big snowstorm this year, she and Annabelle wouldn't be sledding together, and Annabelle wouldn't be spending the night. Just three months ago, Annabelle had moved all the way to California…and Quinn had no idea when they would get to see each other again. That was one of the reasons why Quinn was so grateful for the opportunity to volunteer at the animal shelter. Playing with the kittens always made her laugh, and she loved taking the dogs for walks in the neighborhood. Quinn knew how important it was to shower the shelter animals with lots of love and care while they waited to be adopted. Happy animals were much more likely to be adopted—and happy animals knew that they were loved. Most of all, though, staying busy helped Quinn keep her mind off how much she missed Annabelle.

"Hey, Dad!" Quinn called out as she walked through the front door.

"Hey, Q!" he called back from his office. As an illustrator, Quinn's dad worked from home in an office that was nearly as well stocked as Ms. Morimoto's store.

"Look—my ornaments came!" Quinn announced as she carefully placed the box on the kitchen table.

"Great news," Dad said as he appeared in the doorway. "I had a feeling Ms. Morimoto would come through for you."

"Four days with no school, no homework, nothing but painting..." Quinn said in a dreamy voice. "One more day until Thanksgiving break, and I can't wait!"

She snuck a glance at the clock. Technically, the rule was that Quinn had to finish her homework before she could paint or draw, but maybe Dad would make an exception today.

As if Dad could read her mind, he laughed. "Go ahead, Q," he said. "I don't see why you can't do your homework after dinner today."

"How did you know what I was thinking?" Quinn asked, smiling.

"You got that look in your eyes," he said knowingly. "That *I can't wait to get started* gleam. I recognized it right away."

Quinn crossed the room to give her dad a big hug. "Thanks, Dad," she said. "I promise I'll get all my homework done after dinner. And I'll do the dishes, too!"

"Even better!" Dad joked.

Quinn scooped up the ornaments and hurried back to her room. It was hard for Quinn to keep her desk tidy—it was always cluttered with school papers, pencils, and books—but she kept her art table perfectly organized. When she had the urge to paint or draw, the last thing Quinn wanted to do was waste time cleaning up!

Quinn's acrylic paints were already arranged in rainbow order. She'd picked out a few metallic accent colors, too—silver, gold, and crimson—which shimmered under the bright light as she poured little pools of paint onto her palette. Then Quinn picked out a gold ornament from the box. She stared at it, deep in thought, as she tried to decide what, exactly, she would paint there.

Tap. Tap. Tap.

Quinn didn't even notice that she was tapping the end of her paintbrush against the side of her palette. *The gold ornament reminds me of Annabelle's dog, Bumblebee,* she thought. *But if I paint him, he'll blend right into the ornament.*

But there was no reason Quinn couldn't paint a dark brown dog instead!

Quinn had been painting animals for ages—especially her friends' pets—so it wasn't too hard for her to paint a chocolate-brown version of Bumblebee. She grinned to herself as she made one of the dog's ears flop the wrong way. It made the dog on the ornament look curious and playful—and ready for fun!

I have got *to text a picture of this to Annabelle,*

Quinn thought as she examined her work. But the ornament didn't feel quite finished. There was something missing...but what?

It's not festive enough, Quinn suddenly realized. With quick, sure strokes, she painted a wreath of dark green leaves around the dog's face. Then she added a few bright red holly berries for a pop of color.

"Less is more" was one of those things adults liked to say, and most of the time, Quinn couldn't disagree more. Fewer chocolate chips in a cookie and less frosting on a cupcake were definitely *not* better than the opposite.

But when it came to artwork, Quinn knew it was usually true. Sure, she could add more and more decoration to the gold ornament, but something deep inside told her that it was just right—just the way it was.

And just in time, too, as Dad called to Quinn from the kitchen, "Dinner's ready!"

Quinn carefully nestled the ornament back in the box, with the painted side up so that it wouldn't smudge. One down...eleven to go. Quinn couldn't wait to find out what she'd paint next!

Chapter 2

Quinn leaned close to the mirror as she applied a thin coat of sparkly lip gloss. She didn't usually wear makeup—but this wasn't a usual night. The Twelve Pets of Christmas gala fund-raiser was in just an hour!

Quinn smoothed her hands over her tulle skirt. Tiny specks of glitter were embedded in the purple material so that Quinn's dress sparkled whenever she moved—almost like one of the ornaments she'd painted! Mrs. Alvarez had been delighted by Quinn's ornaments when she'd delivered them the day before. Quinn could only hope that everyone else attending the auction would feel the same way.

"Ready, Q?" Dad called from the hallway.

"Almost!" Quinn replied. Then she rummaged around in her jewelry box, looking for the perfect accessory: her gold locket with the shape of a paw print on the front. When Quinn found the necklace, she clutched it in her palm as she hurried over to Dad.

"You look beautiful, kiddo!" he announced with a big smile. "When did you get so grown-up?"

"*Dad*. Come on," Quinn said—but she smiled all the same. "Can you help me with this?"

"I'll do my best," he replied as he fumbled with the tiny clasp.

"Thanks, Dad," Quinn said after the necklace was on. "*Now* I'm ready!"

"Want to walk?" Dad asked. "I don't think it's too cold tonight."

"Sure," Quinn replied. Their condo was only a couple of blocks from downtown, so just about everything was within walking distance.

The night air was crisp and cool as Quinn and her dad walked toward the Palladium Center, where the gala would be held. To Quinn, everything was sparkling—from the tiny lights that twinkled in the trees to the stars that shone high overhead. She was so excited about the gala that she almost skipped a little as they walked.

Quinn and her dad were among the first guests to arrive. Quinn could hardly believe the transformation that had happened at the Palladium Center in just twenty-four hours. When she'd dropped off the ornaments the day before, the ballroom had been bare and, under the bright fluorescent lights, almost kind of ugly.

But now?

It was one of the most festive and fancy places Quinn had ever been! Each wall was lined with a long table. The table closest to the door had large portraits of each of the Twelve Pets of Christmas— Lobo and Nana; Rufus and Snowdrop; Tops and Tippy; Paisley, Polka, and Dot; Pixie and Applesauce; and of course, Buddy, one of Quinn's favorite pets.

On the right side of the ballroom, the table

was laden with desserts: tiny chocolate-iced eclairs; peppermint-striped candy-cane cookies; cupcakes topped with frosting wreaths and sparkly sugared cranberries. Quinn's favorite, though, were the gingerbread doghouses decorated with every candy imaginable. She gasped in delight when she realized something.

"Dad! Look!" Quinn cried. "There are six doghouses—and each one has a gingerbread dog in front and a gingerbread cat perched on the roof! And—and they're the Twelve Pets up for adoption!"

Dad grinned. "That's some impressive attention to detail," he said approvingly.

Quinn leaned close to each doghouse to get a better look. "Look!" she said. "There's Applesauce and Snowdrop...and this one looks just like Rufus...."

"Quinn!" a voice said.

Quinn spun around to see Ms. Morimoto from the art store. "You came!" she said excitedly. "Thank you!"

Ms. Morimoto smiled. "I wouldn't miss it for the

world," she replied. Then she turned to Quinn's dad. "Hi, Alan. You must be so proud of your daughter."

"Well, of course," Dad replied as he wrapped his arm around Quinn.

"Front and center on the display. You couldn't pay for better placement," Ms. Morimoto continued.

A puzzled look crossed Quinn's face. "What display?" she asked.

"Oh, you haven't seen the display yet?" asked Ms. Morimoto.

Quinn shook her head.

Ms. Morimoto clapped her hands together. "Then there's something you really need to see," she replied. "Follow me!"

The crowd was definitely picking up, but Ms. Morimoto deftly wove her way through all the men and women wearing dressy clothes, leading Quinn to the table on the opposite side of the room. It was clear right away that this table held all the items for the silent auction; Quinn saw enormous gift baskets filled with everything from fancy skin-care products to gourmet chocolates. There were vacations for auction, dinner at the mayor's house, and even a motorcycle! Quinn's smile grew bigger and bigger as she gazed at the generosity of her community. Her ornaments were a small contribution compared to everything else that had been donated, but Quinn was glad she could help, even a little.

Or *had* she helped? She thought her ornaments would've been scattered around the table, but Quinn hadn't spotted a single one yet. *Maybe they had too much stuff,* she thought suddenly. *Maybe all the other donations were so awesome that my ornaments didn't fit in anymore.*

But if that was the case, why was Ms. Morimoto smiling so much?

Then Quinn saw it: In the center of the table, on a beautiful gold pedestal, stood a miniature Christmas tree, decked out with gleaming twinkle lights and—

Quinn gasped—

Her ornaments!

All twelve of them glittered from the tree, catching the light. There was even a sign by the base of the pedestal:

Hand-painted ornaments
by Quinn Cooper
Opening bid per ornament:
$50

"Fifty dollars?" Quinn said in astonishment. *"Each?"*

"And worth every penny," Ms. Morimoto said.

"I just can't believe it," Quinn said, shaking her head. "I thought they'd sell for maybe twenty dollars. But... at least fifty dollars each..." Quinn paused to do the math in her head. "That would be six hundred dollars!"

"It's going to be more than that. Look—you've already got some bids," Dad told her, showing Quinn the sign-up sheet. Sure enough, the blue ornament with a white cat already had three bids... and would be auctioned for at least eighty dollars!

"Quinn! There you are!" Mrs. Alvarez said as she hurried up to the group, beaming. "Not bad, eh?"

"Not bad?" Quinn echoed. "It's incredible—such an honor! Thank you!"

"The minute the decorating team saw your ornaments, they scrapped their original centerpiece plans," Mrs. Alvarez told her. "Who could blame them? Your ornaments perfectly capture the spirit of the Twelve Pets of Christmas. They've got pets, they've got Christmas...."

"They've got glitter," Ms. Morimoto added, winking at Quinn. Everyone laughed.

"I just can't believe people would pay so much for my ornaments," Quinn marveled.

"They're beautiful, Quinn," Mrs. Alvarez told her. "You have a real talent for painting."

"I agree," added Ms. Morimoto. "There's such a lighthearted playfulness in your animals. You've truly captured their unique spirit in each one."

Quinn laughed. "Well, I had a lot of inspiration from the shelter pets," she said.

Mrs. Alvarez glanced at her gold watch. "Speaking of the shelter pets..." she began.

Quinn's eyes lit up. "Is it time?" she asked.

"Just about," Mrs. Alvarez replied, nodding. "You should go ahead and get backstage."

"Backstage?" Ms. Morimoto asked Quinn's dad. But he looked just as confused as she did.

"I have a surprise for you," Quinn said mysteriously. "I'll see you in a little while. Until then... enjoy the show!"

Quinn followed Mrs. Alvarez out of the ballroom and down a long corridor to an empty conference room. Quinn smiled as they approached the door. She didn't need Mrs. Alvarez to lead the way anymore; she could've found it just by listening for the barks and meows that echoed down the hallway!

"This is the holding room," Mrs. Alvarez explained. "I think you and Buddy will be fifth in the lineup."

"Yay!" Quinn cheered. "I get to walk Buddy in the Pet Parade!"

The Pet Parade was the big surprise that Quinn had been keeping for weeks. Because the Twelve Pets of Christmas gala wasn't just for people...it was for pets, too! All twelve pets would be making a special guest appearance in a few moments—and as a shelter volunteer, Quinn had been asked to walk one.

"Ready for the parade?" Mrs. Alvarez asked with a laugh. She held open the door for Quinn, who was delighted to see so many of her animal friends. They'd been dressed up for the occasion, too; each one was wearing a festive velvet bow around his or her neck.

Just then, Buddy came bounding over. Quinn immediately dropped to her knees so she could give him a big hug. "Hi, Buddy!" she cried. "You look so fancy! And you smell so nice, too!"

"All the Twelve Pets were bathed today," Mrs. Alvarez joked. "You should've seen it, Quinn. Bubbles everywhere!"

"Well, I'm sure they all want to put their best paw forward." Quinn giggled.

Buddy tossed back his head and let out a loud, happy bark. He was clearly aware of all the excitement in the air. Quinn understood why. Buddy had already lived at the animal shelter for more than a year. The volunteers tried to give him as many walks—and as much love—as they could, but it was hard to give him the attention he deserved when there were so many other animals in need. Being out of the shelter and surrounded by so many people made this an extra-exciting night for Buddy.

Quinn couldn't figure out why Buddy hadn't been adopted yet. She knew he was a mutt—Mrs. Alvarez thought he had a mix of border collie and golden retriever—and that a lot of people wanted "purebred" dogs. But Buddy had so much to offer! He was friendly to everyone, even the cats, and playful, with a long tail that was constantly going *thump-thump-thump* when he wagged it. And Buddy was smart, too. Quinn could tell from the spark of intelligence that lit up his dark brown eyes and from the way his ears twitched on high alert at the slightest sound.

"Maybe tonight's the night, Buddy," Quinn whispered close to his ear. "Maybe your new family's waiting right out there... and we don't even know it yet!"

Mrs. Alvarez approached Quinn and Buddy, carrying a long red leash. "Ready?" she asked. "It's just about time to line up. The Pet Parade starts in five minutes!"

Quinn stood up abruptly, smoothed out her skirt, and fluffed her hair. Then she clipped the leash to Buddy's collar under the velvet bow. "You look adorable, Buddy," she said.

"And adoptable!" Mrs. Alvarez added with a big smile.

One of the shelter volunteers, Kelli, was lining up the pets and their handlers in the hallway. "Buddy and Quinn," he called out, "you're next!"

Quinn's heart made a funny, fluttery jump in her chest. She didn't have stage fright, exactly—Buddy was the star of this show—but she was filled with so much anticipation that it was no wonder her hands were suddenly trembling.

And Quinn wasn't alone. Buddy was acting more excitable than she'd ever seen him before. His ears were on high alert, and he was sniffing the air like it was chow time.

The first pet, a cocker spaniel named Applesauce, went through the doors.

"You can tell it's a big night, can't you, Buddy?" Quinn said in a low voice as she stroked his silky-soft ears to calm him. Buddy was trembling with excitement. He looked up at Quinn and replied by licking her palm with his slobbery tongue.

Quinn giggled. "Yes, Buddy, I know. I love you, too," she replied.

It was Pixie's turn next. The young cat was wrapped up in a baby blanket in Janelle's arms, purring so loudly that Quinn could hear her.

Now there was just one more pair ahead of Quinn and Buddy—a feisty pup named Lobo and his handler, Lara.

"We're next," Quinn whispered to Buddy. Did he straighten his shoulders, too—or did she just imagine it?

"Quinn and Buddy—go!" Kelli said in a loud whisper.

Quinn's hold on Buddy's leash tightened. A big, beaming smile crossed her face. She shook her hair over her shoulders and, with Buddy by her side, stepped through the doors.

The lights were brighter than Quinn remembered—of course, that made sense since they were pointed right at the stage.

"And now we have faithful Buddy, being walked

by one of our volunteers, Quinn!" Mrs. Alvarez's voice boomed over the speakers. "Buddy is a mix of a bunch of great breeds—border collie, golden retriever, and Labrador, we think, which explains why Buddy is so friendly, loyal, and fun."

Buddy stopped short on the catwalk. He cocked his head. He could hear Mrs. Alvarez's voice—but he couldn't see her.

"Keep walking, Buddy," Quinn said, her teeth clenched behind her big smile. "Everybody's watching us!"

"But what we can't explain is why Buddy has been waiting for his forever family for over a year," Mrs. Alvarez continued. "At the shelter, we try not to pick favorites..."

"Woof!" Buddy barked—a loud, resonating bark that interrupted Mrs. Alvarez mid-sentence.

"But it's no secret how much the staff and volunteers love Buddy," Mrs. Alvarez continued without missing a beat. "And if you adopt Buddy—"

"This way, Buddy!" Quinn said, pulling gently on his leash. All they had to do was make it to the end of the catwalk and back. It wasn't even that far—fifteen steps at the most—

But Buddy wouldn't budge. He could hear one of his people-friends, and now he wanted to find her. Buddy dropped his head to the floor and began sniffing, trying to catch Mrs. Alvarez's scent. His tail wagged back and forth, back and forth, *thunking* into Quinn's sparkly shoes. She laughed nervously as she tried to guide him back onto the path, but suddenly Buddy felt like he weighed about a thousand pounds. The festive bow around his neck began to unravel, leaving a long strand of ribbon that tangled around one of his hind legs.

The people in the audience giggled as they watched Buddy's antics. Nobody was paying much attention to Mrs. Alvarez anymore.

"We promise you won't be disappointed!" Mrs. Alvarez finished. "Let's hear it for Buddy and Quinn!"

As the crowd started to clap, it happened: Buddy spotted Mrs. Alvarez at last. He charged toward her. Quinn's shoes were slippery and she lost her balance, but Buddy didn't notice. He was so excited to run toward Mrs. Alvarez that he just pulled Quinn behind him.

"Buddy! Stop!" Quinn cried. She held on to the leash even tighter—even though it meant getting dragged across the catwalk in her best party dress. Buddy was *her* responsibility, and nothing would make her let go of him now!

Mrs. Alvarez's dark brown eyes widened in alarm. "Buddy!" she said in her warning voice. "Sit! STAY!"

It worked—almost too well. Buddy skidded to a halt, his oversized paws splaying out in four different directions. He slid across the catwalk, still dragging Quinn behind him, until—

Wham! Buddy flew off the edge of the platform and landed in a heap at Mrs. Alvarez's feet. Quinn, still clutching the leash, tumbled after him!

The crowd gasped as several people rushed forward to help Quinn up.

"I'm fine, I'm fine," she assured everyone. Quinn held up her hands, with Buddy's cherry-red leash still wrapped around her palm. "No harm done!"

"Friendly, loyal, and fun—did I tell you?" Mrs. Alvarez announced into the microphone, making everyone laugh as Buddy started licking Quinn's hand. "Quinn, I might add, is the young artist behind the incredible ornaments for auction tonight."

A woman in a pretty silver party dress turned to Quinn in surprise. "You painted all those animal ornaments?" she asked.

Quinn nodded, grinning. Mrs. Alvarez waved to Kelli, who hurried forward to take Buddy out.

"I just *love* them!" the woman gushed. She beckoned to her friends across the room. "Caryn! Jackie! This is the girl who painted the ornaments!"

A few other people turned to look as other women joined the group. Quinn was blushing again. She'd already had enough of being the center of attention for one night.

"Do you take custom orders?" someone asked. "I'd *love* to have my Siamese cat, Cindy Lou, painted on a blue one to match her eyes."

"I—" Quinn began.

"Oh, yes! What a great idea!" another woman exclaimed. "I have two dogs, so I'd want an ornament for each of them, of course."

"This would make a great Christmas present," a

man said. "My mother is *devoted* to her teacup poodle. She never leaves the house without him. And she dresses him in the silliest little sweaters...."

"Put me down for two ornaments, too," another woman chimed in. "How much?"

Quinn's mind went blank. How much? She didn't know where to begin! "I—uh—" she stammered.

Luckily, Ms. Morimoto was nearby. "If you're interested in a custom ornament, please write your email address on this sheet," she said. "The artist will get back to you in a few days with a price quote."

"Thank you," Quinn told Ms. Morimoto as people crowded around to sign up. The Pet Parade was back on; she glanced up at the stage to see one of the volunteers wheeling mama cat Paisley and her kittens, Polka and Dot, in a baby carriage. From the way everyone in the crowd cooed, Quinn could tell that the Twelve Pets gala was a big success.

Now Quinn could only hope that the adoption applications would stack up as fast as the requests for her ornaments!

Chapter 3

After school on Monday, Quinn went to the animal shelter for her volunteer shift. When she opened the door, she was greeted by the festive sound of jingle bells ringing. "That's new!" she exclaimed, looking up to see a strip of brass bells hanging from the top of the door.

"Tommy's home for Christmas break—and he's got a serious case of the Christmas spirit," Mrs. Alvarez said with a laugh. "I don't think we've ever decorated quite so much." Her son, Tommy, was in college, but he helped at the animal shelter whenever school was out.

"I love it!" Quinn exclaimed. The animal shelter had been transformed into a holiday wonderland! Garlands of gleaming tinsel swooped down from the ceiling, and a large, light-up wreath had been hung behind the front desk. Quinn's favorite decorations were in the waiting area, though. The rows of plastic chairs had been replaced with some comfy chairs, and Tommy had added an electric fireplace next to the window, complete with stockings that hung above the glowing embers. A light-up Hanukkah menorah adorned the shelf above the fireplace. There was even a table with milk and cookies for Santa—but instead of cookies, the platter held dog biscuits!

"Where did this furniture come from?" Quinn marveled.

Mrs. Alvarez smiled. "My sister runs a secondhand shop," she explained. "Tommy had this great idea to turn the waiting room into a living room for the holidays, so Maritza gave him a few pieces that haven't sold. I like it a lot, actually....Maybe we should keep it like this, even after the holidays are over."

"Definitely!" Quinn agreed. "It would be nice for

people to visit with animals here when they're deciding whether to adopt. It feels more like home."

"And it makes the whole shelter look nicer," Mrs. Alvarez said. "Which is good, because I think things are going to be *very* busy this month! Did you see yesterday's newspaper?"

Quinn shook her head.

"We made the front page!" Mrs. Alvarez told her as she held it out to Quinn. Sure enough, there was the headline—THE TWELVE PETS OF CHRISTMAS ARE WAITING FOR YOU—and a large photo of Mrs. Alvarez as Lobo and Lara walked in the Pet Parade.

"I'm just glad they didn't use a photo of me falling on my face," Quinn joked.

Mrs. Alvarez's expression grew serious. "How are you feeling? Any bumps and bruises today?"

"Nope. I'm totally fine," Quinn assured her. "And, actually, I think maybe it was a really good thing!"

"Really?" replied Mrs. Alvarez.

"Yeah. I mean, if Buddy hadn't dragged me off the catwalk and made that big commotion, people might not have realized that I painted the ornaments," Quinn explained. "I got *forty-seven* orders!"

"Are you kidding?" Mrs. Alvarez exclaimed.

"I couldn't believe it, either!" Quinn said. "Ms. Morimoto helped me figure out how much I should charge. She said that artists shouldn't give their work away for free, so we calculated how much the supplies would cost, and how long it would take me, and how much people wanted to buy them—she said that was *demand*—"

"I love it!" Mrs. Alvarez said. "I'm so proud of you, Quinn! Look at you, with your own art business now!"

"I definitely want to donate half of the proceeds to the animal shelter," Quinn said.

Mrs. Alvarez reached over to give Quinn a hug. "Are you sure, sweetheart?" she asked. "You've already given the shelter so much."

"I'm positive," Quinn replied firmly. "But...if it's okay with you...would you mind if I kept the rest of the profits for myself?"

"Of course that's okay!" Mrs. Alvarez said right away. "Are you saving up for something special?"

Quinn's eyes shone with excitement. "Yes!" she exclaimed. "Right before school started, my best friend, Annabelle, moved to California. If I can get all forty-seven ornaments painted before Christmas, I think I'll be able to afford an airplane ticket to visit her during spring break!"

"That's wonderful, Quinn!" Mrs. Alvarez told her. "I know how much you must miss your friend. And I bet she misses you, too."

Quinn nodded. "Anyway—how can I help today?" she asked.

"Let's see...." Mrs. Alvarez said thoughtfully. "We gave all the cages a deep clean over the weekend, and the animals were groomed on Friday...."

"Inventory?" Quinn guessed. "Do you want me to count all the pet food in the storage room?"

"I have a better idea," Mrs. Alvarez said. "I'll tackle the inventory. Why don't you work on some socialization? Especially for the Twelve Pets."

"My favorite job!" Quinn cheered. She knew that whenever she volunteered at the animal shelter, she needed to do whatever task she was assigned. But it was no secret that Quinn loved playing with the animals more than anything. And it turned out socializing was the most fun job, too. It involved everything from teaching puppies how to walk on a leash to cuddling itty-bitty kittens. Most of all, it helped animals learn how to be friends with people— and how to be loved.

"Thanks, Quinn," Mrs. Alvarez called as Quinn headed off toward the cat wing. She walked down the aisle between the cages, trying to figure out which animal to play with first. Everyone liked to play with mama cat Paisley and her kittens, Polka and Dot; from the way all three were sleeping, Quinn could tell they'd been tired out. Rufus, a big orange cat, opened one eye and yawned in Quinn's face as she walked by. "Okay, okay," she giggled. "Go ahead and get your beauty sleep!"

Since so many cats were snoozing, Quinn made her way to the dog wing. A pair of dogs, Tops and Tippy, were out on a walk—Quinn could see that one of the other volunteers had signed them out.

Then Quinn saw Buddy, and her heart did that funny flip-flop. He was curled up in a corner of the cage, staring at the wall, not showing even the tiniest bit of interest in the footsteps coming his way.

Just like that, Quinn's decision was made.

She strode over to Buddy's pen and let herself in. "Hey there, Buddy," she crooned.

Thump-thump-thump!

Buddy perked up right away. In half a second, he was on his feet, that wildly wagging tail thumping against the wall of his pen. He bounded over to Quinn and nudged her with his head.

"I'm glad to see you, too!" Quinn laughed. But at the same time, she was a little worried. As she'd walked down the hall, Buddy hadn't even bothered to look up to see who was coming his way. She knew why. After living in the shelter for so long, Buddy knew better than to get his hopes up when a person walked in.

But just because no one had adopted him yet didn't mean that no one ever would. And if Buddy didn't show any interest in the visitors to the shelter... would they show any interest in him?

Quinn sighed as she stroked Buddy's head. He really was a great dog. How could she help others see the Buddy she knew so well?

Then she heard the bells ringing.

Someone had opened the front door!

Chapter 4

"Hang on," Quinn promised Buddy. "I'll be right back!"

She slipped out of Buddy's pen and hurried toward the door. A middle-aged woman and her son were standing near the front desk, looking around.

"Welcome to the Marion Animal Shelter," Quinn said brightly. "How can I help you?"

"We're getting a dog!" the little boy yelled gleefully, jumping up and down so much that his red baseball cap fell off his head.

"Whoa, whoa, whoa," his mom said, laughing as she held up her hands. "Let's settle down a little, Charlie."

Quinn smiled. "Would you like to meet some of our animals?" she asked. "I can give you a tour."

"Thanks," the woman replied. "I'm Ms. Ferrino. And this is my son, Charlie."

"I'm Quinn. I've been volunteering here since September," Quinn replied. "Mrs. Alvarez, the director, is here, too—she'll be back in a minute if you have any questions about the adoption process."

"Where are the dogs? Can I pet them?" Charlie asked, starting to jump up and down again.

"Easy, cowboy," Ms. Ferrino said, making Quinn laugh.

"They're right this way," Quinn told Charlie. "Have you ever had a pet dog before?"

"No, but I've always wanted one," Charlie replied. "I love dogs! If we had a dog, it could sleep in my bed, and I would walk it four times a day and feed it good food and we would be best friends."

Charlie's enthusiasm made Quinn smile even

bigger—but something in Ms. Ferrino's face gave her pause.

Ms. Ferrino gently laid her hand on Charlie's shoulder and said, "Remember what we talked about," in a low voice.

Charlie's feet stopped jumping. He nodded. Now Quinn was even more confused.

"Sorry about that," Ms. Ferrino explained. "I should've mentioned this earlier.... The dog isn't actually for us."

"Oh," Quinn replied. "So you're just...visiting?"

"Actually, my work is interested in adopting a dog," Ms. Ferrino explained. "I'm a nurse's aide at Candlewick Assisted Living Community. We've been talking a lot about adopting a dog for the residents. The companionship would be great for them, but a dog is too much responsibility for them to handle on their own."

"It *is* a lot of work—especially walking them during the winter," Quinn said, nodding in agreement.

"But I know our residents miss having pets," Ms. Ferrino said. "A dog for them to pet and play with would make Candlewick feel even more like home."

"What an awesome idea!" Quinn said. She started racking her brain, trying to think which dog at the shelter would be the perfect fit. "Is there any specific type of dog you have in mind?"

"Well..." Ms. Ferrino began.

"Puppy! Puppy! Puppy! Puppy!" Charlie cheered.

Ms. Ferrino wrapped her arm around his shoulders. "We can look at the puppies today, but I think they might be a little too energetic for our residents," she replied. Then she turned back to Quinn. "Maybe a midsized dog—not too big," she continued. "And not a puppy, but on the young side."

"Personality?" Quinn asked.

"Gentle, definitely," Ms. Ferrino said. "And loving and kind. Most of our residents enjoy a quieter lifestyle—and we'd want a dog who could adapt to that."

"That makes perfect sense," Quinn said. "Let me introduce you to some of our dogs! We're also having a special promotion right now—the Twelve Pets of Christmas—"

"Oh, yes!" Ms. Ferrino said. "I heard an ad on the radio about it. In fact, that's what made me decide to stop by today after I picked up Charlie from school."

Yes! Quinn cheered to herself. But she wanted to act as professionally as Mrs. Alvarez, so she just smiled and said, "Great! Then you already know that if you adopt one of our featured pets, there's a discount on the adoption fee. Now, this is where our dogs and puppies live until they find their 'furever' homes. If you want to meet anybody, just let me know."

Quinn had watched Mrs. Alvarez give tours often enough that she knew when to step up—and when to stay out of the way. That's exactly what she did, giving Ms. Ferrino and Charlie a chance to explore a little on their own. If they had trouble, Quinn would be happy to offer suggestions. But usually, people were able to find the perfect pet on their own.

Thump-thump-thump!

Quinn perked up immediately. She knew exactly what was making that thumping noise—Buddy's tail as it started wagging! Could this be it? Had Buddy found a family at last? It wasn't exactly the kind of home Quinn had imagined for him...but maybe having a lot of older adults to dote on him was exactly what Buddy deserved after all the time he'd spent at the shelter.

"Mom! Mom!" Charlie called out. "I like this one! Can we meet him?"

"Okay," Ms. Ferrino called back.

Quinn stepped forward to open Buddy's cage. He bounded right over to Charlie and licked the side of his face. Charlie dissolved into giggles as he nuzzled Buddy's soft fur.

And Buddy? He'd never looked happier!

"He seems like a nice dog," Ms. Ferrino said. "How old is he?"

"We're not exactly sure," Quinn began, "but our vet thinks he's probably seven or eight years old."

Ms. Ferrino's face fell a little. "Oh."

Quinn knew that wasn't a good sign. "He's a *great* dog," she said quickly. "One of my favorite dogs *ever!*"

Ms. Ferrino smiled kindly. "I can tell!" she replied. "But we were hoping to adopt a younger dog for Candlewick. It's going to be a very different environment there, you know. It might be too much for an older dog to adapt to."

Quinn nodded slowly. That made sense—even if it wasn't the answer she wanted to hear. *Remember, we want to find the best pet for every situation*, she reminded herself. *Not force something that isn't meant to be.*

"We have a lot of other dogs who are looking to be adopted," Quinn said. "How about…let's see… maybe Nana?"

Ms. Ferrino laughed. "Nana? We already have a lot of Nanas at Candlewick," she joked. "And Grandmoms, and Grammies, and Pop-Pops, and Grandpas…"

Quinn laughed, too. "Nana is named after the dog in *Peter Pan*," she explained. "You know, the one who takes care of Wendy and her brothers? But you can change her name, of course."

"Come on, Charlie," Ms. Ferrino said. "Let's go meet this Nana dog."

A flicker of disappointment crossed Charlie's face. "Can I hang out with Buddy?" he asked. "Look— I think he likes me!"

"Oh, he definitely likes you," Quinn told Charlie. It was undeniable—from the way Buddy had rolled onto his back so Charlie could scratch his tummy to the way Buddy's tongue was lolling out of his mouth. Buddy was clearly smitten with Charlie.

"Nana's actually just two pens down," Quinn explained. "She's a three-year-old golden retriever mix and she's so sweet! We started calling her Nana because she likes to take care of the other animals. Sometimes the new dogs are really scared when they first arrive, and Nana always wants to cuddle up to them and help them feel safe."

"Really?" Ms. Ferrino said. "That's incredible!"

"Here she is," Quinn said as she opened Nana's pen. "Nana! Come say hi!"

Ms. Ferrino knelt down and held out her hand. "Hi, Nana," she said in a soothing voice.

Nana rose to her feet, wagged her tail, and nuzzled Ms. Ferrino's hand. Ms. Ferrino's smile grew.

"Wow, she really is a sweetie," Ms. Ferrino said as she stroked Nana's silky coat.

"I'll let you get to know her a little better. Let

me know if you need anything," Quinn said as she stepped back to check on Buddy and Charlie. She recognized that look on Ms. Ferrino's face, though—and she had a feeling that Ms. Ferrino and Nana were going to be just fine.

Back in Buddy's pen, Buddy had sprawled across Charlie's lap. Charlie didn't seem to mind, though. He was busy telling Buddy all about his favorite video game.

"How's it going?" Quinn asked as she sat down next to Charlie.

"Good!" Charlie replied. "Buddy and me are friends now."

"I can tell," Quinn said. "You're great with dogs. So, do you have any pets at home?"

Charlie shook his head. "But my uncle has a dog, Smoky, and he lets me take care of him whenever we go to his house," he said. "And one time when my uncle went on a business trip, Smoky got to stay at our house for three days!"

"Wow!" Quinn said. "I bet you had fun!"

"We had the *best* time," Charlie replied. "I took

really good care of Smoky. And I learned a lot about having a dog."

For a moment, no one spoke.

"Maybe someday I'll get to have my very own dog," Charlie said.

"I'm sure you will," Quinn replied. "And when you get a little older, you can help out at the shelter— just like me! And then you can play with dogs whenever you want."

Charlie's face lit up, just as Ms. Ferrino walked up to them.

"So how did—" Quinn began…but she didn't need to finish her sentence. One look at Ms. Ferrino's smile told her all she needed to know.

"I think we found Candlewick's newest resident!" Ms. Ferrino announced happily. "Nana is the perfect dog for us. I know everybody—residents and staff— will love her as much as I do!"

"That's awesome!" Quinn cheered. "If you'll just follow me, you can fill out an application. It only takes a day or two to process, and then your adoption will be final."

"Mom?" Charlie spoke up. "Can I stay here... with Buddy?"

Ms. Ferrino faltered for a moment. "Um—sure—if it's okay with Quinn, I guess...."

"Fine with me," Quinn said quickly. Charlie and Buddy looked so happy together. In fact, they looked like they belonged together.

Chapter 5

At school the next day, Quinn made sure to get to her art class as early as possible. She needed to ask Mr. Spaulding for a favor—a *big* favor—and she wanted to make sure she got off on the right foot.

The art studio was all set up to begin a new unit: sculpture. There was a slab of damp clay at each workstation, along with an assortment of cool-looking tools, including hooks, loops, and dowels. They seemed really interesting, and Quinn was so eager to try sculpting that she almost reconsidered her special request.

Almost.

The students started filing into the room, each one choosing a different workstation. One of Mr. Spaulding's rules was that everyone had to switch seats at the start of a unit. "Artists need to see the world from all different angles," he had said. "You don't want to get stuck in the same old seat, staring at the same old things."

Eliza Evans, one of the most popular girls at Marion Middle School, dropped her backpack at the workstation next to Quinn's.

"Hey," Quinn said with a little wave.

"Hey," Eliza replied. She glanced curiously at the box on Quinn's workstation. "What's that? An early Christmas present?"

"Not exactly," Quinn said, giggling. "It's actually—"

Just then, Mr. Spaulding entered the room. Quinn grabbed the box and got up so fast that her chair screeched across the floor. She knew she had to catch Mr. Spaulding quickly, before he started class, if she wanted to make her special request.

"Mr. Spaulding?" Quinn asked as she hurried up to the teacher. "Can I talk to you for a minute?"

"Sure," he replied as he reached for his art apron. "Is everything okay?"

"Yes," Quinn replied. "I just—I was hoping I could ask you a favor."

Mr. Spaulding raised an eyebrow as he nodded at her. "Go ahead."

"Would it... would it be okay if I work on my own project during the sculpture unit?" Quinn asked, the words tumbling out in a rush. "I could make up the sculpture work during Christmas break so that I don't miss out."

Mr. Spaulding frowned. "I have a pretty strict policy about this sort of thing, Quinn," he began. "If one student wants to get out of a unit, the next thing you know, *everyone* wants to skip out on the assignment."

Quinn's heart fell. *I guess I shouldn't be surprised,* she thought. *I can't imagine any other teacher letting me off the hook.*

"But I have been known to make exceptions in exceptional cases," Mr. Spaulding continued. "Why do you need to work on an original project during class time, Quinn?"

Quinn opened the red box to show him the ornaments. "Over Thanksgiving, I painted a bunch of ornaments to benefit the Marion Animal Shelter," she explained. "And it turns out they were a really big hit! I got forty-seven custom orders at the gala last Saturday!"

"Wow!" Mr. Spaulding replied. "Impressive—and unsurprising. These look great, Quinn. You should be very proud."

"Thank you," Quinn said, beaming from the praise. "The only problem is—that's a *lot* of ornaments. And my dad says I have to finish my homework before I can paint them at home."

"Very sensible," Mr. Spaulding said, nodding.

"And I guess I just feel a lot of pressure to get all the ornaments finished before Christmas," Quinn continued. "Especially since I'm going to donate half of the profits to the animal shelter."

Mr. Spaulding tapped his chin thoughtfully. As Quinn waited for him to respond, she started to feel a teeny, tiny, itty-bitty flicker of hope.

"You make a compelling case," he finally said. "This certainly is a time-sensitive art project, and for a *very* good cause. A cause that's close to my own heart, I should add. I adopted my cat, Penny, from the Marion Animal Shelter nine years ago."

"You did?" Quinn exclaimed.

"Can't imagine life without Penny," Mr. Spaulding said, chuckling to himself. "Yes, Quinn, you have permission to paint ornaments during class time, with the expectation that you will complete the sculpture unit on your own time during the holiday break."

"Thank you!" Quinn exclaimed happily. "I promise I'll work extra hard on my sculpture project! I'll—I'll even do extra-credit assignments!"

Quinn scurried back to her seat as Mr. Spaulding began to teach the class about sculpture. His introductions to a new topic always included a Power-Point slide show, which gave Quinn time to gather all the supplies she would need to paint ornaments instead of sculpt clay. She could tell that the other students were watching curiously as she put away the clay tools and got out her paintbrushes. Even Eliza at the next workstation was intrigued.

At the end of Mr. Spaulding's presentation, the

students started working with the damp, heavy clay—except for Quinn.

"No clay?" Eliza asked in a low voice. "How come?"

In a hushed whisper, Quinn told her all about the ornament-painting project.

"That's incredible!" Eliza said when Quinn finished. She looked genuinely impressed.

"Thanks," Quinn replied. "I really love being a volunteer at the shelter, and I wish I could help all the animals there find homes. So I'm glad that the ornaments can help pay their expenses. It gets *really* expensive to take care of so many animals. You wouldn't believe how much food Mrs. Alvarez has to order every month. And the vet gives her a pretty big discount but, you know, medicines and surgeries and checkups can get really expensive."

"I didn't know kids were allowed to volunteer at the animal shelter," Eliza said.

"You have to take a special class and get permission from your parents," Quinn explained. "It's one of my favorite things to do. I've loved animals ever since I was little....I used to have this big plan to have twenty pet cats!"

"Twenty pet cats!" Eliza said, cracking up.

Quinn smiled sheepishly. "I know—crazy," she replied. "I think that's when my dad started introducing me to art. Twenty paint sets is a lot easier to handle."

"Oh, I'm not laughing at you," Eliza said quickly. "I'm laughing because I had a plan like that when I was little, too. I wanted to have an orange cat, a gray cat, a tabby cat, a tuxedo cat...."

Quinn started to laugh. "A cat collection!" she said.

"Collect them all!" Eliza added, laughing even harder.

"Girls..." Mr. Spaulding said in a warning voice.

Quinn and Eliza immediately stopped laughing and got back to work. Mr. Spaulding liked it when students enjoyed art class...but he never hesitated to let them know when they were having a little too much fun.

"So what kinds of things do you do at the shelter?"

Eliza asked. "Is it, like, cleaning cages and scooping litter boxes?"

"Sometimes," Quinn admitted. "But most of the time, I get to play with the animals so that they learn how to trust people. Sometimes I answer the phones or file paperwork. It depends on what Mrs. Alvarez needs on any particular day."

"My parents and I have been talking about getting a cat," Eliza said thoughtfully. "I mean, *they've* been talking about a cat; I've been *begging* for a cat."

Quinn stifled her laugh. "I know what that's like," she said. "I begged my dad to let us adopt our cat, Piper, for, like, six months."

"They're not sure I'm *responsible* enough yet," Eliza said, rolling her eyes. "But how can I show them how responsible I am if they won't give me a chance to prove it?"

"I know, right?" Quinn exclaimed. Then she had an idea. "You know, if you adopt a pet from the shelter and it doesn't work out, you can return it for up to a year."

"Really?" Eliza looked surprised. "People *do* that?"

"Sometimes," Quinn said. "I mean, obviously it's not ideal, and that's not what anybody ever wants, but sometimes it just isn't a good match."

"That's so sad."

"It is. But what I mean is—you could tell your parents that if you don't take care of the cat, they can bring it back to the shelter," Quinn said.

"That's actually genius," Eliza said. "I wonder if they'll go for it."

"Doesn't hurt to try," Quinn replied.

"I mean, I get why my mom doesn't exactly want to add 'scooping a litter box' to her daily to-do list," Eliza said. "She's crazy busy with work and stuff already. But I don't think I'd mind it that much."

"It's really not that bad when you get used to it," Quinn told her. Then she had an idea. "Why don't you visit me at the shelter some afternoon?"

Immediately after she said it, Quinn felt weird. Had she really just invited the most popular girl in seventh grade to hang out with her at the animal shelter?

"Not, like, for litter box cleaning lessons or anything," Quinn plowed on, feeling dumber with every word. "Just to play with some kitties. Oh! We have a mama cat and two kittens right now. They are *so* cute! You will *love* them. I mean, if you want to stop by sometime. Or not."

"Yeah," Eliza said, nodding. "That sounds cool. I've never been to the animal shelter before, actually. I'd like to check it out. When do you volunteer?"

"It kind of depends on how much homework I have," Quinn replied. "But I'm probably going tomorrow afternoon. And maybe again on Friday."

"Cool," Eliza said. "I'll try to come by."

"Seems like you two are enjoying your new workstations," Mr. Spaulding said lightly. That was another clue that Quinn and Eliza were chatting a little too much.

"Sorry," Quinn replied before turning all her attention to the ornament she was painting, a turtle on a metallic green globe. She knew that Mr. Spaulding had given her a special opportunity to work on her ornaments during class time…and she didn't want to blow it!

❄ ❄ ❄

The next afternoon, Quinn looked up every time she heard the jingle bells on the door ring, certain that the next person who came into the shelter would be Eliza. But each time, she was wrong. It was getting a little silly—it seemed like those bells were ringing every few minutes, yet each time she heard them, Quinn jumped. After she'd been volunteering for almost two hours, though, Quinn had to face the truth: Eliza wasn't going to show up.

Maybe she forgot, Quinn thought. *Maybe she's cramming for a big test.* But the one thought Quinn didn't want in her mind—that Eliza had blown her off—kept creeping in uninvited. Quinn tried to shrug it off. If Eliza didn't want to visit the cats—or hang out with her—there was nothing Quinn could do about it.

Even if it did make her feel kind of lousy.

The bells jingled again. Again, Quinn looked up. It still wasn't Eliza—but it was someone else she knew.

"Hey, Charlie!" Quinn exclaimed. "What's up?"

"Today's the big day," Ms. Ferrino announced as she walked in behind her son. "Mrs. Alvarez called this morning to tell us that Nana's adoption has been approved!"

"Yay!" Quinn cheered gleefully. Adoption days were the best! "Let me get Nana's going-home bag together."

Charlie tugged on his mom's sleeve. "Can I see Buddy real quick?" he asked. "To give him the... *surprise*?"

Ms. Ferrino glanced at her watch.

"Please?" Charlie begged. "I just want to say hi. He's my new best friend!"

Mrs. Alvarez walked behind the counter. "Quinn, you can take Charlie back to see Buddy. I'll take care of everything up here," she said.

"You got it," Quinn replied. "Come on, Charlie! Let's go see Buddy B!"

"Why do you call him Buddy B?" Charlie asked as Quinn brought him back to Buddy's pen. "Does his last name start with B?"

Quinn shook her head. "Buddy doesn't have

a last name," she said. "It's just a silly nickname I made up."

"If Buddy came to my house, his last name would be Ferrino. Like me," Charlie said.

Quinn chose her next words very carefully. "Do you think that's something that might happen?" she asked.

Charlie, his eyes gleaming, nodded. "I hope so," he confided. "I wrote a letter to Santa Claus and told him all about Buddy. So maybe..."

"Maybe!" Quinn replied.

Thump-thump-thump!

Buddy's wild wagging tail was at it again.

"Okay, you two," Quinn said as she opened up the pen. "Have a nice visit!"

"Buddy!" Charlie exclaimed gleefully. He burst into the pen and threw his arms around Buddy's neck. "I missed you, boy! Did you miss me? I brought you a present! It's a squeaky Santa!"

Quinn stepped back, keeping an eye on Buddy and Charlie through the glass windows of the pen. They were having a great time playing with the chew toy Charlie had brought—when he tossed it into the air, Buddy grabbed it and shook his head back and forth, making the rubber Santa go *sqqqqquuuueak-sqqquuuueak!*

Watching them play, Quinn had that funny feeling again that maybe, just maybe, Buddy had found his family after all.

Even if they didn't know it yet.

Chapter 6

Quinn was so busy with homework and ornament-painting that she didn't volunteer at the shelter again until Friday afternoon. When she walked inside, it felt like she had stepped into a big party! Mrs. Alvarez and Tommy were wearing shiny party hats and laughing happily with two people Quinn didn't know.

"Hey, what did I miss?" Quinn joked as she hung up her coat.

"Rufus is being adopted today!" Mrs. Alvarez announced. "Meet Juniper and James. They just opened the new bookstore on Grove Street."

"Rufus? That's awesome!" Quinn exclaimed. "Congratulations! He is *so* funny."

"Rufus definitely has a big personality," Mrs. Alvarez told his new owners.

"We can tell," James replied, rubbing his stubbly chin. "When we came yesterday, he locked eyes with us and started yowling and yowling. It was like he was trying to say, *Hey, you guys, I'm right here!*"

Everyone laughed, especially Quinn. James had described Rufus perfectly—which gave her a good feeling that this adoption would work out just fine.

"Even before we opened our bookstore, we agreed that it would need a cat," Juniper said. "Bookstore cats are pretty fantastic."

"When people see a cat in a bookstore, they get so excited," James said.

"Rufus is going to love hanging out at your store," Quinn said. "He *adores* people. Spending all day with customers is going to be a dream come true for him."

James and Juniper exchanged a grin. "I knew we had a lot in common," James joked.

"We're both pretty loud and opinionated, too," Juniper added. "So we thought Rufus would fit right in."

"And we *love* parties," James continued. "Rufus's adoption seemed to call for a celebration, so we brought the hats."

"And cupcakes!" Tommy said as he offered one to Quinn.

"You want a hat?" James asked Quinn.

"Sure!" she replied, plucking a metallic fuchsia hat from the stack on the desk.

"I'll get Rufus," Mrs. Alvarez said. "This party needs its guest of honor!"

A couple of minutes later she returned, her arms full of a giant orange cat. Rufus's long, fluffy tail flicked back and forth. He opened his mouth to meow, but a big yawn escaped instead, making everyone laugh.

"You want a party hat, Rufus?" James said.

"No, he's way too dignified for that," Juniper protested. She took Rufus from Mrs. Alvarez. "Aren't you, Sir Rufus von Ruffington?"

"Oh, yeah, that's really dignified," James teased his wife.

The jingle bells rang again.

"Welcome to the party!" James called out.

"Uh—hi—sorry, are we interrupting?" a tall man asked.

"Not at all! The more the merrier," Juniper said. "We're having an adoption party for my new friend, Roo-foo."

"Roo-foo?" James groaned. "That's even worse."

"Roo-foo disagrees," Juniper said in a serious voice. "Can't you hear how loudly he's purring?"

"How can I help you?" Quinn asked as she hurried over to the man.

"I'm here for an adoption, too," he said. "A puppy? Lobo?"

"Oh!" Quinn cried. "I love Lobo! I'm so happy for you! He's the cutest!"

The man grinned. "Thanks! I can't wait to take him home."

"Hey, would you mind taking a picture of us?" Juniper asked the man. "We want to get this all over social media and introduce Roofy-poofy to our customers."

"Sure," the man replied. "Everybody squeeze together."

Quinn ducked out of the picture just in time. "Mrs. Alvarez will finish processing your forms—I'll go get Lobo," she said.

Quinn couldn't help humming some Christmas carols as she went back to the dog pens. *Two adoptions in one day?* It was incredible! And proof that the Twelve Pets of Christmas promotion was working!

Nana, Rufus, and Lobo—three pets since the gala, Quinn thought. At this rate, all the animals would be adopted before Christmas for sure!

Just as that thought crossed her mind, though, Quinn saw Buddy, all curled up in the corner of his cage. He lifted his head a tiny bit as she walked past. His tail went *thump*—but just one time.

A pang of sadness hit Quinn hard. "Poor Buddy," she whispered to herself. She wondered if he was missing Charlie. Had Buddy given up hope that Charlie would come back? The squeaky Santa toy was tucked under one of Buddy's legs, almost like he was holding on to a stuffed animal.

Quinn glanced over her shoulder. The sound of laughter drifted down the hallway from the lobby, where the adoption party was still in full swing. She knew that nice man was waiting for Lobo...but maybe he could wait for just a few more minutes.

She slipped into Buddy's pin and knelt beside him. "Don't worry, Buddy," she said. "I *promise* somebody's going to adopt you. It's only a matter of time, and then you'll have a family of your very own again! And it will be incredible!"

Thump. Thump.

Two tail wags—a slight improvement.

"And I'm going to do everything in my power to make it happen," Quinn vowed.

Ting-a-ting-a-ting!

The bells on the door were jangling again!

Oh, boy. Here we go, Quinn thought as she hurried out of Buddy's pen. She rushed over to Lobo's pen, scooped him up, and then hurried back to the lobby to greet the newcomer. Quinn was in such a rush that she skidded across the shiny polished floor and would have collided right into Lobo's new owner if she hadn't grabbed the counter just in time!

"Whoa! Sorry!" Quinn cried as she placed Lobo into his new owner's arms. Lobo recognized the man at once and covered his face with slobbery doggy kisses.

"Congratulations on your new puppy!" Quinn told him. Then she turned to the door...and saw Eliza standing there!

"Oh! Hey!" Quinn exclaimed.

"Hey," Eliza replied with a little wave. "Sorry I didn't make it earlier this week. My ice-skating practice ran long every day."

"Ice-skating? That's cool," Quinn said. "I didn't know you were into that."

"Yeah, I've been skating for a while now—since third grade," Eliza said. "Most of the competitions are out of town, though, so people don't really know about them."

"That's too bad," Quinn said. There was a pause while she tried to figure out what to say next.

"Well, my mom's just finishing a phone call in

the car," Eliza finally said. "But she said I could go ahead and start looking at the pets."

"You mean she said yes?" Quinn cried in excitement.

Eliza, her eyes shining, nodded. "Not only that, but she filled out an adoption application last week!" she said. "Mom says we're already approved!"

Quinn gasped. "That's amazing!" she said.

"It was supposed to be a Christmas surprise," Eliza said sheepishly. "But I kept bugging Mom and Dad...and Mom finally told me everything and said I could help pick out our new pet!"

"I'm so excited for you!" Quinn exclaimed. The image of Buddy curled up in a corner of his pen flashed through her mind, and she remembered the promise she'd made to him.

"I have the *perfect* pet for you," Quinn continued. "His name is Buddy, and he's the most amazing dog. Everyone here adores him!"

But Eliza shook her head. "Cat, remember?" she said. "We're going to get a cat."

"Oops, I forgot," Quinn said. "Would you like to meet Buddy anyway?"

Again, Eliza shook her head. "I wish I could," she said. "I'd actually love to have a pet dog. But I'm allergic."

"I'm sorry," Quinn told her. "I didn't know. The good news is we have *tons* of cats! And I can show you the kittens, too, even though they're not quite big enough for adoption... and Mrs. Alvarez likes to send kitten siblings home in pairs, if she can...."

Eliza laughed. "I can ask my mom if she'll let me adopt two kittens—but I'm pretty sure she'd say, 'Don't push your luck.'"

"Don't worry, we have plenty of other cats," Quinn assured her. "The kitty section is this way. Follow—*whoa!*"

At that moment, Lobo wriggled to the ground—and ran right for Eliza! Quinn tried to block the eager puppy, but he was too fast. The next thing she knew, he was jumping and prancing around Eliza, placing his little paws on her knees and yipping excitedly.

"Aww!" Eliza cooed. "What a cute little sweetie!" She knelt down, partly to pet Lobo and partly to gently move him away.

"Here—let me—*Lobo! Down!*" Quinn said, using the firm voice that Mrs. Alvarez had taught her. As Rufus started yowling loudly, Lobo only got more riled up.

At last, Quinn managed to scoop up Lobo. "Sorry about that," she apologized to Eliza as she handed Lobo back to his new owner.

But it was too late. Eliza's eyes were already watering, and before she could reply to Quinn, she sneezed!

"Uh-oh," Eliza said between sneezes.

Quinn's hands flew up to her mouth. "Are you okay?" she cried.

"I'll—*ah-choo!*—be—*ah-choo!*—fine—*ah-choo!*" Eliza sneezed.

"Do you—do you need to leave?" Quinn asked, worried.

Eliza shook her head and stifled another sneeze. "I'll probably be okay when we see the cats," she answered, rubbing her itchy eyes. "There aren't any dogs in the cat section, right?"

"No, none at all," Quinn assured her. "The cats would never allow it."

"Then I'm sure I'll be fine in a minute or two," Eliza said.

Just to be on the safe side, Quinn grabbed a handful of tissues from the counter as she hurried Eliza over to the cat wing. Eliza's sneezing slowed down once they were away from the dogs, but she kept rubbing her eyes.

"They're so beautiful," Eliza said as she peeked in each cat cage. "How can anyone pick just one?"

"It's not easy," Quinn told her. "But I've seen it happen so many times: All of a sudden, there's, like, this spark...this connection...between a person and a pet, and that's it—an adoption about to happen. If you see a cat you'd like to pet or play with, just let me know. We have a visiting room where you can hang out."

"I guess 'all of them' isn't really helpful, is it?" Eliza asked with a laugh.

Quinn just smiled as her classmate wandered down the hall. Suddenly, Eliza stopped. "Oh! The kittens!" she said in a loud whisper.

"The mom is called Paisley, and the kittens are Polka and Dot," Quinn told her. "The kittens are so funny! They get crazy, jumping and pouncing all over for like thirty minutes...and then they flop over and fall asleep at the same time."

Eliza looked a little disappointed. "I must have just missed their playtime," she said.

"Don't worry, you can come back anytime to play with them!" Quinn replied.

The girls continued down the hall, pausing every few steps so Eliza could peek into one of the cages. She paused at Snowdrop's cage. "Wow, she's beautiful," Eliza breathed. "Can I pet her?"

"Of course," Quinn said. She opened the cage and reached in for Snowdrop. The fluffy, long-haired cat was easy to handle, and she started purring almost the moment Quinn placed her in Eliza's arms.

A smile of pure happiness spread across Eliza's face. Quinn smiled, too. She recognized that look. She'd seen it just about every time someone decided to adopt a pet.

"The visiting room is at the end of the hall," Quinn told Eliza. "You and Snowdrop can hang out for a while and get to know each other. It's got some toys, too—a feather on a string and a catnip mouse and—"

"*Ah-choo!*" Eliza suddenly sneezed. "Sorry! I think I must still have some dog fur on my clothes. I should probably get home and change...and take a shower...."

"Of course," Quinn replied. She was a little surprised by the sudden turn of events. Quinn had felt so sure that Eliza would want to adopt Snowdrop. "Here—let me help you put Snowdrop back in her cage."

"Actually," Eliza began, "I was hoping I could take her home with me."

"Yes! I knew it!" Quinn cheered. "A perfect match!"

"Really?" Eliza asked. "How did you guess?"

"You got that special look on your face," Quinn explained. "That's when I knew!"

Eliza started to say something, but a sneeze cut her off. A worried expression crossed Quinn's face.

"Let's get you out of the shelter," Quinn told her. "I'll put Snowdrop back in her cage until your mom can come in and finish the adoption."

"Thanks," Eliza said, wiping her watery eyes with a tissue. "I can still take Snowdrop home today, right?"

"Sure," Quinn told her. "After all, your parents' application has already been approved. We even have a spare cat carrier you can borrow to take her home."

After Snowdrop was back in her cage, Quinn and Eliza returned to the lobby. Lobo and his new owner were still there, which made Eliza sneeze even harder! Someone else was in the lobby, too—Eliza's mom.

"Uh-oh," Mrs. Evans said, looking concerned. "I was worried about this."

"Mom! I found the perfect kitty!" Eliza cried. "Her name is Snowdrop and she's the sweetest thing ever, with the prettiest fur and bright green eyes—"

"Is she the one?" Mrs. Evans said, equally excited.

Eliza nodded vigorously. "Wait until you meet her! She's perfect!"

"Or *purr*fect?" joked Mrs. Evans.

The girls laughed—until Eliza's laugh turned into a sneeze.

Mrs. Evans rummaged around in her purse. "I brought your allergy medicine—I had a feeling you might need it this afternoon," she said. "Here, Eliza, why don't you take my keys and wait in the car. I can finish up the adoption paperwork."

"Thanks, Mom," Eliza said. "And thanks, Quinn! I love Snowdrop already. See you on Monday!"

"See you," Quinn said as she walked Eliza to the door. "I hope you feel better soon."

"I will," Eliza assured her. "My allergy medicine works pretty fast."

After Eliza left, Quinn went back to the counter. Mrs. Alvarez had already started completing Snowdrop's paperwork. "Quinn, you can get Snowdrop ready to go," Mrs. Alvarez said.

"You got it," Quinn replied. She found the spare carrier in the storage closet and brought it to Snowdrop's cage. The cat immediately arched her back when she saw it—a warning sign that Quinn recognized right away.

"Don't worry, sweet girl," Quinn said in a soft, soothing voice. "I promise you this is a car ride you *definitely* want to take. Because you know what's waiting at the other end? Your new home—and your new family!"

Snowdrop knew Quinn—and she trusted her. After Quinn stroked Snowball's back and scratched under her chin, the skittish kitty was calm enough to be placed in the carrier. Quinn felt a little pang as she carried Snowdrop to the waiting room. She was beyond glad that Snowdrop had found a family... but Quinn was going to miss seeing her all the same. *At least I know Snowdrop's new owner.* Quinn tried to console herself. *When I see Eliza at school, I can ask how Snowdrop is doing. Maybe Eliza will even show me pictures of Snowdrop on her phone!*

"Here she is!" Mrs. Alvarez announced as Quinn and Snowdrop entered. "The paperwork's all done. Congratulations on your new cat, Mrs. Evans."

"Thanks for all your help," Mrs. Evans replied.

"Good luck," Quinn said as she passed the cat carrier to Mrs. Evans. "I hope Eliza's feeling better soon."

Ding!

Mrs. Evans paused to read a text on her phone.

"Oh, Quinn—would you give me your phone number?" she asked.

"Sure," Quinn replied. "If you have any questions or problems getting Snowdrop adjusted, you can call or text me anytime."

"Thanks—that's a very nice offer," Mrs. Evans said. "But Eliza wants your cell so she can invite you over to hang out—and play with Snowdrop."

Quinn tried to hide her surprise. "Oh! Sure! That would be great," she said. "I was just thinking about how I was going to miss seeing Snowdrop around here."

"I don't think you'll be missing her for long," Mrs. Evans said with a smile. "Eliza was hoping you could come over this weekend. But she'll text you all the details later, I'm sure."

"That would be awesome," Quinn said. "Bye, Mrs. Evans. Bye, Snowdrop! See you soon!"

The bells jingled merrily as Mrs. Evans carried Snowdrop's carrier into the frosty evening air. The sun had started to set, casting deep blue shadows over the parking lot. Quinn stood there for a moment, watching Mrs. Evans load Snowdrop into the car and marveling at everything that had happened.

Three pets adopted in one afternoon—Rufus, Lobo, and Snowdrop!

And an invitation to hang out at Eliza's house!

It was definitely shaping up to be a Christmas season full of surprises!

Then an image of Buddy, curled up all alone in his pen, popped into Quinn's mind. Her smile faded.

Would it turn out to be a season of Christmas miracles, too?

Chapter 7

A few days later, Quinn was back at the animal shelter, working on desk duty while Mrs. Alvarez helped the vet perform routine checkups on some puppies who'd been found behind a grocery store. Quinn would've liked to help, too, but Mrs. Alvarez was really strict. She never let any of the junior helpers near the animals until the vet had given them a clean bill of health—just to be on the safe side.

Quinn glanced up when the bells on the door rang. "Hey, Charlie. Back again?" she teased when she saw Charlie's familiar red baseball hat. At this point, she would've been surprised if Charlie *hadn't* come to visit Buddy. He faithfully arrived promptly at 3:29—right after the elementary school got out— every day after school. Mrs. Alvarez told Quinn that he'd visited Buddy over the weekend, too. He'd even taken the official adoption photo of Mr. DeLorio and his new kitten, a gray ball of fluff named Pixie.

"Yeah. Me and Buddy got to a really exciting part of our book yesterday," Charlie told her. "I promised Buddy I wouldn't read the next chapter without him. The waiting is killing me!"

"Wow! You're a true friend," Quinn said. "Don't let me hold you up. I'm sure Buddy's dying to know what happens next, too."

Just as Charlie began to head back to Buddy's pen, Quinn called after him. "Hey, Charlie—guess what?"

"What?" he asked.

"We've got *five* new puppies!" she exclaimed. "Dr. Trazler is giving them checkups right now, but if you want to peek through the exam room window, you could see them!"

Charlie smiled, but he shook his head. "That's okay. Maybe next time," he told her. "Buddy's waiting for me."

"Of course," Quinn said. "I know you don't want to keep Buddy waiting."

She watched Charlie hurry down the hall toward Buddy's pen. Charlie didn't even need Quinn to let him in anymore. He practically knew enough to be a junior volunteer himself.

Quinn had just returned to filing paperwork when the bells jingled again.

"Hello?" a young woman called out as she entered. She was wearing blue scrubs, and that was probably why Quinn recognized her so quickly.

"Dr. Lu!" Quinn exclaimed as she got up from the desk. "Hi! How are you? I'm surprised to see you!"

The doctor looked confused for a moment.

"My name's Quinn. You took care of me in the emergency room two years ago when I broke my arm," Quinn continued. She held up her left arm and wiggled it around. "You did a great job, too."

A look of recognition flashed through Dr. Lu's eyes. "Of course! I remember now. A waterslide accident, right? Your best friend and her mom brought you in?"

"Yes!" Quinn cried. "That's right!" She'd never

forget how worried Annabelle had been. She'd refused to leave Quinn's side. Even when Quinn had to get an X-ray, Annabelle waited in the hall and talked to her the whole time.

Quinn shook her head, as if to clear away the memory and focus on the present. "I'm one of the volunteers here. How can I help you?" she asked Dr. Lu.

"I'm interested in adopting a pet, I think. But it's kind of a specific situation," Dr. Lu replied.

"Okay," Quinn replied. She grabbed a pen and a piece of paper so she could take notes. "Tell me more."

"My mother's going to move to Marion," Dr. Lu explained. "She lives in Texas right now, and ever since my dad died a few years ago, she's been really lonely. So we thought it might be a good idea for her to move here so she could be closer to family.

"The only problem is that I have to work really long shifts a few days a week," she continued. "When I'm on call, I might have to stay at the hospital for twenty-four hours or longer. I hate the thought of my mom sitting alone in the house for hours and hours and hours."

"So are you thinking of getting a companion animal?" Quinn asked.

"Yes, exactly," Dr. Lu replied. "And to be honest, I've wanted a pet for a long time myself! But it wouldn't have been fair to bring a pet into my home, not with a work schedule like that."

"So the right pet will be good for your mom... and for you," Quinn said.

"That's what I hope," Dr. Lu replied. "It's kind of silly...."

Quinn waited while Dr. Lu tried to find the right words.

"When I was a kid, we had to move to a new state for my dad's job," Dr. Lu continued. "I was so unhappy about leaving all my friends, and my school, and my bedroom. But my parents surprised me with a puppy when we got to our new house. It was the best surprise ever! Sparky was my best friend. Eventually, I made friends with kids at my new school, but Sparky made the transition so much easier. So I guess I'm hoping a new dog will help my mom as she gets used to the move."

Quinn picked up on the word "dog," which led to her next question. "Do you have a preference for a dog or a cat?"

Dr. Lu looked thoughtful. "A dog, I guess," she replied. "We always had dogs when I was growing up. I wouldn't know the first thing about taking care of a cat!"

Quinn made a few notes. "Anything else I should know?" she asked.

"We probably can't handle a puppy," Dr. Lu told her. "So a calmer, adult dog would be great. Preferably one who's already been trained. And a smaller dog is a good idea, too, since my mom will be responsible for taking him or her out when I'm at work."

Quinn paused. "Do you live in a house or an apartment?" she asked.

"A house," Dr. Lu replied.

"What about the backyard? Is it fenced?" Quinn asked.

"Yes," Dr. Lu said. "My hope is that Mom will take our dog for walks in the neighborhood when it's nice out. But at night, or when it's raining or snowing, she can just open the back door to let the dog out."

"Sounds good," Quinn replied. "Would you like to meet some of our dogs?"

Dr. Lu nodded. "Yes! I'm excited! And I know Mom will be, too—if we find the right one."

The right one.

That was the challenge, wasn't it? Sometimes, a match happened easily. Other times—not so much.

Quinn racked her brain, trying to anticipate which dog would be best for Dr. Lu and her mom. She'd already said no puppies, so the new pups were out of the question. And she wanted a smaller dog, which meant that Buddy wasn't the right one, either. And neither was Tops, an enormous bullmastiff. There was another reason why Tops wouldn't be right—he had a very special dog friend, Tippy, an itty-bitty West Highland terrier. Dr. Trazler called Tops and Tippy a bonded pair, which meant that they needed to stay together, no matter what. It was usually harder to find someone who was willing to adopt more than one animal at a time, but in the case of Tops and Tippy, Quinn knew that Mrs. Alvarez would never separate them. They didn't just love each other—they needed each other.

"Applesauce!" Quinn said suddenly.

Dr. Lu gave her an odd look. "Sorry?" she said. "What did you say?"

"You should meet Applesauce," Quinn said, beaming. "She's the sweetest little cocker spaniel! She's four years old and very well trained. And she weighs about twenty-five pounds, so she's not too big."

"A cocker spaniel?" Dr. Lu repeated. "They're great dogs. Yes, I'd love to meet her."

"Follow me!" Quinn sang out.

As they walked through the dog area, Quinn snuck a glance at Buddy's pen. Charlie was sitting with his back against the wall, Buddy's head in his lap. He held his book with one hand as he read, while using his other hand to pet Buddy. They looked so content together, a perfect fit.

"That's wonderful," Dr. Lu said.

"What is?" asked Quinn.

Dr. Lu gestured toward Buddy's pen. "I didn't know the shelter has a reading program for pets," she said. "I read an article about it online a while ago. It's such a cool idea. Kids get to practice their reading skills, and animals get companionship and affection while they wait to be adopted."

"It *is* a great idea," Quinn said, nodding in agreement, "but we don't have a program like that here.

That little boy just really, really likes that dog. He comes almost every day."

"Aww," Dr. Lu said. "How sweet."

"I'll tell Mrs. Alvarez about that reading program, though," Quinn continued. "I bet a bunch of kids would like to read to our animals. Well—here's Applesauce!"

When she heard her name, Applesauce popped up and trotted over to the door, wagging her short, stubby tail.

Quinn watched Dr. Lu out of the corner of her eye. There it was—the widening smile, the gleaming eyes. Quinn had a good feeling about this match—a *very* good feeling. She opened up Applesauce's pen and clipped a leash on Applesauce's collar.

"We have a visiting room over here," Quinn told Dr. Lu. "You and Applesauce can hang out for as long as you want. There's a button on the wall—see it?— that you can push when you're ready for me to come back."

"Thanks so much for your help, Quinn," Dr. Lu replied. "I think Applesauce and I are going to get along just fine."

Quinn was grinning as she headed back to the front desk. She stole one more look at Charlie and Buddy, who seemed happier than ever. There was just one thing wrong with that picture, though: Buddy and Charlie should be hanging out in Charlie's home, sprawled on the couch together. Not crouched on the hard floor of the animal shelter.

Quinn didn't want to disturb them—but she couldn't resist. She tapped softly on the door to Buddy's pen, then let herself in.

"How's it going?" she asked Charlie. "Do you need anything?"

Charlie, smiling, shook his head. "Nope," he replied. "Me and Buddy are great. All we need is each other."

"I can tell how much Buddy loves you," Quinn told the little boy. "I think you're his favorite person ever!"

It was the right thing to say; Charlie's smile grew even bigger.

And then Quinn blew it.

"Do you think your family might adopt Buddy?" she asked.

Charlie's smile vanished in an instant. "No," he said in a small, sad voice.

Quinn waited for him to continue, but Charlie didn't say anything else. She felt like she'd made a huge mistake—but how? It was a simple question. Anybody who saw Charlie and Buddy together would want to know if the Ferrino family was going to adopt Buddy.

"Well," Quinn said, forcing herself to sound cheerful, "you can visit Buddy whenever you want!"

"Thank you," Charlie replied. His voice still sounded very small.

Quinn slipped out of Buddy's pen and closed the door behind her. *I just don't get it*, she thought, shaking her head. It was so *obvious* that Buddy and Charlie were meant to be together. And Charlie's mom liked dogs.... She'd come to the shelter to adopt one for her workplace and obviously enjoyed spending time with the pups.

So what was the problem?

The question was still on Quinn's mind when she got back to the front desk, where Mrs. Alvarez was finishing up a phone call.

"How are the new puppies?" Quinn asked when Mrs. Alvarez hung up.

"A clean bill of health!" Mrs. Alvarez announced. "They're just adorable, too…a pack of roly-poly fluffballs. Dr. Trazler wants them in quarantine for another week, but after that I think they'll find homes fast."

"That's great," Quinn replied. And it was—but she couldn't help thinking that it was a little, well, unfair. The puppies had just arrived, and they'd probably all have new homes by the end of the month.

But Buddy had been waiting for *months*—over a year. Where was his forever family? When would it be his turn?

"Something wrong?" Mrs. Alvarez asked lightly. Quinn realized that her expression must've given away her thoughts.

"I was just thinking about Buddy," Quinn said with a sigh. "He and Charlie are total besties. But Charlie says they're not going to adopt him. Why?"

There was a strange look on Mrs. Alvarez's face. Quinn didn't know what it meant.

Then Mrs. Alvarez sighed. "Quinn, I'd like to tell you something in confidence," she began. "Do you know what that means?"

"Super-secret, private info?" Quinn guessed. "Never to be repeated?"

"Pretty much," Mrs. Alvarez replied.

Quinn waited expectantly for Mrs. Alvarez to continue...though suddenly, she wasn't quite sure she wanted to know what Mrs. Alvarez was going to tell her.

"Charlie and his mom can't adopt Buddy because they can't afford him," Mrs. Alvarez said in a low voice.

Quinn blinked. She knew that having a pet was expensive—in fact, one of the saddest reasons why people gave their pets over to the shelter was because they could no longer afford to take care of them—but she hadn't expected that to be the case for Charlie and his mom. After all, Ms. Ferrino had a job! Her job at Candlewick Assisted Living was the reason Charlie and Buddy had even met each other.

"But—" Quinn began.

"I saw what you saw in Buddy and Charlie,"

Mrs. Alvarez continued. "The perfect match. I was so excited! I thought, at *last*, our sweet Buddy had found his forever family."

Quinn nodded. She'd thought so, too.

"But as the days passed, and Ms. Ferrino didn't ask about adoption papers for Buddy, I got a bad feeling," Mrs. Alvarez said. "So a couple of days ago, I decided to ask her myself. That's when she told me that she went back to school in September."

"Back to school?" Quinn repeated.

Mrs. Alvarez nodded. "Right now, she's a nurse's aide," she told Quinn. "But when she graduates, she'll be a nurse practitioner—and able to earn a lot more money. In the meantime, though, things are going to be pretty tight for her and Charlie. Higher education doesn't come cheap. There's tuition, books, supplies...not to mention times when Ms. Ferrino will have to work a little less to focus on her studies."

Quinn was starting to understand—not that it made it any easier. "So they can't adopt Buddy right now," she said slowly. "But after Ms. Ferrino graduates, they'll have more money, right? How long will that take?"

"Two years," Mrs. Alvarez replied. "But there's good news here—because Ms. Ferrino already said that as soon as she finds a new job, she and Charlie will adopt a dog for sure!"

Quinn barely heard that last part, though. After Mrs. Alvarez said "two years," it was like her ears shut down. "Two years?" she repeated incredulously. "Two *years*? But Buddy can't wait that long! He's already so sad and lonely!"

Mrs. Alvarez chose her next words carefully. "Well, Quinn, of course the hope is that Buddy will be adopted long before then," she said. "Just because the Ferrinos won't be his forever family doesn't mean he won't find a different one."

"You mean separating Buddy and Charlie?" Quinn asked slowly. The thought was almost worse than imaging Buddy living in the shelter for two more years.

"I know it's not ideal," Mrs. Alvarez replied gently. "But ultimately, the best thing we can hope for Buddy is that he finds a loving home as quickly as possible. Right?"

Quinn nodded without saying a word. The big lump that had formed in her throat made it hard to speak.

"And even though that won't be Charlie, look how much Buddy has gotten from his visits," Mrs. Alvarez continued. "And I think Charlie's gotten a lot from Buddy, too."

Quinn tried to smile.

"Sometimes it's not easy to work or volunteer here," Mrs. Alvarez said. "Sometimes things don't work out quite the way we hoped. But that's the thing, Quinn—there's always hope. There's hope for every single animal we take care of. And hope for every single person who comes through that door."

Just then, the buzzer rang. Quinn jumped. "That's Dr. Lu," she exclaimed. "She's been getting to know Applesauce."

Mrs. Alvarez raised her eyebrows. Quinn saw a flash of the hope she'd mentioned.

Mrs. Alvarez pressed the button on the wall and leaned close to the intercom. "How's it going?" she asked.

Dr. Lu's voice crackled over the speaker. "I'm ready to adopt Applesauce! What do I need to do next?"

"That's wonderful news!" Mrs. Alvarez replied,

grinning at Quinn as she made the thumbs-up sign. "Quinn will be right there to get Applesauce so you can fill out some paperwork."

Quinn tried to match Mrs. Alvarez's enthusiasm. It really *was* great news that Applesauce would have a home of her very own. But Quinn couldn't shake the feeling that it was always the other dogs who got lucky...and never Buddy.

"Don't give up on Buddy," Mrs. Alvarez told Quinn, as if she could read her thoughts. "I still believe the right family will find him. It's just taking longer than we would like."

"I won't give up," Quinn replied.

But as she hurried down the hallway to get Applesauce, Quinn couldn't bear to even glance in the direction of Buddy's pen, where he and Charlie were having so much fun together. She thought about how hopeful she'd been the other day—that maybe a Christmas miracle was possible for Buddy *and* Charlie.

Now, though, Quinn had to admit...maybe not.

Chapter 8

The moment the bell rang after school on Monday, Quinn powered up her cell phone. Her fingers drummed the desk excitedly as she waited for an Internet connection. On Mondays and Thursdays, there was this perfect window of time—immediately following school for Quinn and right before lunch for Annabelle—when the girls could text for a few minutes. Quinn looked forward to it all week.

Annabelle: Q??? you there???

Quinn: yes heyyyy! How r u?

Annabelle: pretty good. We started swimming today in PE my hair is like dripping everywhere

Quinn: PE?

Annabelle: Gym. They call it Physical Education here

Annabelle: guess i'm picking up the language lol

Annabelle: so what's up with u???

Quinn: Busy busy busy. Off 2 shelter in a min

Annabelle: aww! Adopting lots of pets??

Quinn: yup!

Quinn: 12 Pets of Xmas is going so great! 5 pets adopted, 7 2 go

Annabelle: yayyyyy! Did u get my msg last nite?

Quinn: not until this morning. Sorry i didn't call u back. Is everything ok?

Annabelle: yeah. i have a super special surprise for you for xmas

Quinn: you don't have 2 get me anything!

Annabelle: too late and IM NOT TELLING

Quinn grinned as she read Annabelle's text. Then she started typing.

Quinn: Surprise sounds good. I have one 4 u 2. It's not big so don't get 2 excited or anything

Quinn couldn't help giggling to herself. Technically, a plane ticket *wasn't* that big—even if a trip to California would be!

Annabelle: Ooh ooh ooh is it one of your ornaments? With bumblebee's picture painted on it?

Quinn: I'll never tell

Annabelle: fine be that way. Are u going caroling soon

Quinn: probably but it won't be the same without u

Annabelle: well duh. How could it be. Lol

Quinn: seriously tho. i miss you. Let's video chat soon.

Annabelle: next weekend?

Quinn: for sure. I gotta get to the shelter... mrs. alvarez is expecting me...

Annabelle: bye q catch you later

Quinn: byeeeee

Quinn tucked her phone in her pocket, still grinning. Annabelle was going to be *shocked* when she told her about the plane ticket! All her hard work painting ornaments was paying off, too. She only had about ten more to paint before she would earn enough for a ticket to California!

When Quinn arrived at the shelter, though, she could tell something was wrong. Mrs. Alvarez and Tommy were staring at the computer with worried looks on their faces. They didn't even notice when Quinn walked in.

"Hey," she said awkwardly. "Um—is everything—"

Mrs. Alvarez looked up and managed a smile. "Hi, Quinn. How was school today?" she asked.

Quinn shrugged. "It was good. How is everything here?"

Tommy's forehead was wrinkled from his deep frown. "You want to tell her, Ma, or should I?"

"Tell me what?" Quinn asked nervously. Was one of the animals sick? Or—Quinn didn't want to think about it—had one of the recent adoptions failed?

"It's the kittens." Mrs. Alvarez sighed. "We had a

lot of visitors over the weekend, and some adoption inquiries for the kittens."

Quinn was surprised. "But—that's good news, right?"

"Two kittens. Two families," Tommy explained. "We tried to convince them to take the pair together—or take a kitten and their mama—but nobody would budge."

"Wait a minute," Quinn began. "You mean split the kittens up? Split all three of them up?"

Mrs. Alvarez nodded.

"No!" Quinn exclaimed. "We can't do that! They're too young! They're—"

"They *are* young, but not too young to be adopted," Mrs. Alvarez replied. "They've been eating kitten food for a couple of weeks now, and they're in great health. Dr. Trazler checked them on Friday. No, we don't have a good reason to prevent their adoptions."

"How about keeping a family together?" Quinn asked hotly. "I think that's a good reason."

Tommy and Mrs. Alvarez looked at her, surprised. Quinn felt her face flush.

"Sorry," she mumbled. "I didn't mean it like that. I just—"

"We agree a hundred percent, kiddo," Tommy said. "Nobody wants to see them split up. I mean, just look at them—the kittens fall asleep in their mother's arms, for Pete's sake."

Quinn nodded. She'd seen them do that before. It was the cutest thing in the world—and all the proof she needed that the kitty family should stay together.

"There has to be a way!" she exclaimed.

Mrs. Alvarez looked thoughtful. "If someone else put in an adoption application for all three before the kittens' adoptions were finalized..." she mused.

Quinn's heart leaped. "Is that all?" she asked. "We just need to find someone willing to adopt all three?"

Tommy and Mrs. Alvarez exchanged a look.

"I mean—I know that's still a challenge," Quinn continued. "But...it's also a chance. Please—can I have a few days? I'll do everything I can to find a family who will take all three of them. Please let me try at least."

"I suppose I could just happen to lose these other applications," Tommy joked.

Mrs. Alvarez swatted his hand away from the forms. "No—none of that," she scolded him playfully. "Though it may take me a little longer than usual to check all their references. It *is* a very busy time of year around here."

"Thank you, Mrs. Alvarez," Quinn said gratefully. "I'll get started right away—unless—do you need me to help with something else at the shelter today?"

Mrs. Alvarez shook her head. "No, Quinn, go ahead and work on finding a family for the kittens and their mama," she replied. "This needs to be our top priority."

Quinn nodded, then hurried toward the cat wing. She glanced in to see the two kittens in a playful mood, pouncing and leaping as they tried to catch their mother's twitching tail. Then Paisley pulled the kittens close and started to groom them, licking their faces with her pink tongue. The kittens closed their eyes; Quinn could just imagine the sound of their happy purrs.

Whatever it takes, she promised herself. Then she pulled out her phone and sent a text to Eliza. It was only two words, but it said everything:

KITTEN EMERGENCY!!!!!

❄ ❄ ❄

Fifteen minutes later, Eliza arrived. Her cheeks were pink and she was out of breath from running through the frosty afternoon air.

"I'm here. What's going on? How can I help?" she panted.

"Thanks so much for coming," Quinn replied. "It's—come on, let's talk in the cat visiting room."

To Quinn's surprise, though, the cat visitation room wasn't empty. Ms. Ferrino was there, studying from an enormous textbook.

"Oh! Sorry!" Quinn exclaimed. "I didn't know anyone was in here."

"No, *I'm* sorry," Ms. Ferrino said. "I don't want to be in the way. I've been trying to get a little studying done while Charlie spends time with Buddy. Mrs. Alvarez said I could use any empty room."

"You don't have to go," Quinn said quickly as Ms. Ferrino began to pack up her notes and books. "We'll find another place."

Ms. Ferrino smiled wryly. "To be honest, I was needing a brain break anyway," she said. "Have you ever studied so hard it feels like your brain's about to melt out of your ears?"

Quinn and Eliza nodded in sympathy. "Maybe once or twice," Quinn said.

"A week!" added Eliza, laughing.

"So what's going on with you two?" Ms. Ferrino said. "You looked so serious when you burst in here.... I was a little worried."

Eliza turned to Quinn. "Yeah, tell it all," she said. "Your text left me with, like, a hundred questions."

"It's Paisley and the kittens," Quinn explained. "If we can't find someone to adopt them all, they're going to be split up!"

Eliza sucked in her breath sharply. "No! That's too sad!" she replied.

"That's why we can't let it happen," Quinn said firmly. "We've got to find a way to keep them together—which means finding a family willing to adopt all three of them."

Eliza turned toward Ms. Ferrino. "I don't suppose you'd be interested in adopting some cats?" she asked hopefully.

No! Quinn wanted to yell. She didn't want Ms. Ferrino to feel like she had been put on the spot. Besides, if the Ferrinos adopted anyone, it should be *Buddy.*

"I wish we could," Ms. Ferrino said, choosing her words carefully. "But now isn't the right time to add a pet to our family—especially not three pets at once."

Eliza wasn't fazed. "Well, I had to try," she joked.

"That's the spirit," Ms. Ferrino told her. "There's no harm in asking! But we'll also need to get the word out...."

Quinn's face brightened. "Do you want to help?" she exclaimed.

"Sure—if you want me to," Ms. Ferrino replied. "I feel like I owe the Marion Animal Shelter such a debt. The residents at Candlewick just adore Nana, and Charlie loves spending time with Buddy."

"You don't owe us anything," Quinn said. "But we could definitely use the help. If we can't find a family to adopt all three of them in the next few days..."

Quinn's voice trailed off, and she could see from Eliza's and Ms. Ferrino's faces that she didn't need to finish her sentence.

"So! Spreading the word," Ms. Ferrino said, getting back to business. She opened her notebook to a fresh page. "I can take a photo of Paisley and her kittens looking adorable and upload it. If people share it around social media..."

"Yes!" Quinn exclaimed. "And I was thinking we could make a flyer to post around town. There's a copy machine in the office and I know Mrs. Alvarez won't mind if we use it to make a bunch of copies."

"Maybe we could put a picture of the kitty family on it, too," Eliza suggested.

"That's an awesome idea!" Quinn said. "We can't print them in color, but maybe if it's a really clear pic it won't matter. I was also thinking of offering three free custom ornaments to anyone who adopts the whole family. There's a special word for that, but I forget what it is."

"Incentive," Ms. Ferrino chimed in. "And I think that's a great *incentive*, Quinn!"

"Yeah, everybody has been talking about your ornaments," Eliza added. "My mom wants to order one with Snowdrop on it."

"Wow—of course! I'm happy to add Snowdrop to the list," Quinn said, grinning. Suddenly her face lit up. "Hang on—I'll be right back!"

A few moments later, Quinn returned. Her arms were full—of kitties!

"Awww! They're here!" Eliza crooned.

"This is the mama, Paisley," Quinn said, placing a beautiful calico cat in Eliza's lap. "And this is Polka"—Quinn paused as she handed an orange-striped kitten to Ms. Ferrino—"and his sister, Dot."

Quinn gave Dot a kiss on her forehead. She tried not to play favorites, but the pure white kitten with a big orange spot on the back of her head—and a striped orange tail—had always held a special place in her heart.

"They are such loves," Ms. Ferrino said, laughing as Polka tried to climb up her sleeve.

Quinn reached behind her and opened a drawer

that was stocked full of cat toys. "Polka! I've got a mousey! Come get it!" Then she tossed a catnip mouse across the floor. There was a furry blur as Polka and Dot raced after it. But the kittens weren't paying attention to where they were going. They skidded across the floor—and crashed into each other! Everyone cracked up.

"A photo is not even going to capture this level of cuteness," Eliza announced.

"Agreed. Maybe I should post a video instead," Ms. Ferrino said, nodding.

"Too bad we don't have any money," Quinn said. "Can you imagine if we made a commercial with these crazy kitties?"

"That would be the best commercial ever," Eliza said, giggling.

And that was all it took for Quinn to have another amazing idea. "Maybe the kitties can be their own commercial!" she exclaimed.

"What do you mean?" Eliza asked.

Quinn gestured to the kittens, who were playing tug-of-war over a feather toy. "They do this all day long," she explained. "It's like constant cuteness, cranked up to level eleven on the cute scale. But nobody gets to see it because they're back here in the cat wing."

"Go on," Ms. Ferrino said encouragingly.

"What if they were on display?" Quinn continued, still figuring out her plan even as she tried to explain it. "Not here—the animal shelter is a little too far out of the way. But if they could be in, like, a store window downtown..."

"It's the last weekend before Christmas," Ms. Ferrino said.

"People are going to be shopping like crazy!" Eliza exclaimed.

"Right?" Quinn said. "So if we could get one of the stores downtown to let Paisley, Polka, and Dot hang out for a few hours... and they were all putting on their cute show..."

"You will get so many applications," Eliza predicted. "Mrs. Alvarez will probably have to shut down the shelter, because there won't be any pets left."

Quinn laughed. "That would be crazy," she told her new friend. Then she turned to Ms. Ferrino.

"Tell me honestly...is this a stupid idea? Is there any chance it could actually work?"

"There's *always* a chance," Ms. Ferrino said firmly. "Now we just have to find a store that would let us do it. The restaurants are out—that would be a health department violation...."

"The post office?" Eliza guessed.

"What about that place that sells handmade vases and necklaces and stuff?" Quinn asked. "They're really busy during the holidays."

Ms. Ferrino nodded slowly. "Yes—that's the right track," she replied. "But I'm not sure that's the right store. So many fragile and breakable items..."

"You're right," Quinn admitted. "I didn't even think of that. If Polka and Dot escaped from the window display and ran wild through the store..."

"*Cata*strophe!" Eliza cried, clapping her hands over her mouth as she burst into laughter. Even Ms. Ferrino started to laugh at the thought.

Suddenly, Quinn's eyes grew wide. "The bookstore!" she exclaimed.

"The new one that opened last month?" asked Ms. Ferrino.

"Yes!" Quinn said eagerly. "The owners were here last week. They love cats—they adopted Rufus to live in the store—oh, I hope they say yes!"

"What are you waiting for?" Eliza asked Quinn, giving her a gentle nudge. "Go! Call them! Call them right now!"

Quinn grabbed her phone and hurried back to the front desk so she could pull Rufus's adoption paperwork and call his owners. She was so excited that she didn't even realize she was holding her breath.

On the third ring, Quinn heard a familiar voice. "Hello, this is Turn the Page! How can I help you?"

It was Juniper!

"Hi, is this Juniper?" Quinn asked in a rush. "This is Quinn Cooper from the Marion Animal Shelter."

"Oh, hi, Quinn!" Juniper said brightly. "Are you calling about my new best friend, Roofy-poofy? He's doing great!"

"That's awesome!" Quinn exclaimed. "How does he like the bookstore?"

"He *loves* it," Juniper replied. "He likes to perch on top of the bookshelves and watch people coming and going. And every afternoon, he curls up in the sunny window and purrs and purrs. You should follow our page online; we post pictures of him every day!"

"That's so cool," Quinn said. "I'll definitely follow your page."

"We're going to start a new thing, 'Reviews by Rufus,'" Juniper continued. "Of course, James and I will be the ones writing the book reviews, but we'll make it sound like Rufus is writing them. Isn't that funny?"

"Yeah, that's hilarious," Quinn replied—but she was still thinking about the sunny front window Juniper had mentioned. "So, I'm really glad to hear that Rufus is doing so well…but I was calling for another reason."

"Oh—okay," Juniper said. "Go on."

"I actually need to ask a favor," Quinn said. "Do you remember those kittens we have for adoption?"

"Of course," Juniper said. "They're so precious."

"Well, we're desperately trying to find a home for them," Quinn began. Then she told Juniper the whole story.

Quinn had barely finished speaking when Juniper rushed to answer. "Of *course* the kittens can hang out in our front window this weekend!" she exclaimed. "We're happy to help find them a home! I'm with you—we've got to keep those sweet babies together."

"Thank you *so* much!" Quinn exclaimed gratefully.

"As soon as we hang up, I'm going to talk to James," Juniper said. "He handles all the displays and decorations. I'm sure he will come up with something fantastic for the front window."

"Really?" Quinn said.

"You know what? I bet we could live-stream it on our website!" Juniper exclaimed. "Everyone will tune in to see the kittens in the bookstore display! This could totally go viral!"

"I hope so! Then we'll definitely find a home for Paisley, Polka, and Dot!" Quinn replied.

"We'll do everything we can," Juniper promised. "Can you bring the kittens over on Saturday morning? Maybe around nine-thirty?"

"We'll be there," Quinn said. "Thank you so much, Juniper! This is going to be great!"

Quinn slipped her phone into her pocket and hurried back down the hall. There were photos to take...posters to draw...signs to hang...and not a moment to lose!

❄ ❄ ❄

On Saturday morning, Quinn and her dad picked up the kittens bright and early. Mrs. Alvarez had already placed them in a carrier with Paisley. The kittens didn't quite know what to make of the strange box with small holes cut into the sides.

"Don't be scared, kitties," Quinn whispered to them as she stuck her index finger through one of the slits. "Today is going to be an adventure!"

One of the kittens nudged her finger—then licked it with a scratchy tongue. Quinn knew that kitten kisses were a good sign.

"Thank you for setting this up, Quinn," Mrs. Alvarez said. "I'm *very* optimistic."

"So am I," Quinn replied. "Don't forget to check the bookstore website. Juniper said they would live-stream the kittens all day!"

"Wouldn't miss it!" Mrs. Alvarez said.

As Quinn was leaving, a couple came in with their young daughter. "Hi. We were wondering if we could meet some of your puppies," the man said.

"Oh! We have a great dog who's ready to be adopted!" Quinn spoke up. "His name is Buddy. And I'll tell you a little secret: He's one of the best dogs *ever*. Like in the history of the whole world."

Quinn smiled brightly and waited for the family to respond. While it would be heartbreaking for Charlie and Buddy to be separated, it would be even more heartbreaking for Buddy to spend the next two years at the shelter—without a family and home of his very own.

"What do you think, sweet pea?" the mom asked her daughter. "Want to meet a dog named Buddy?"

But the little girl stuck out her lower lip and shook her head back and forth. "Puppy," she said firmly. "Want a *baby* puppy."

The parents smiled apologetically at Quinn. "Sorry. She's just had her heart set on a puppy," the dad said as they walked toward the front desk.

Quinn understood—kind of. People wanted what

they wanted, and you couldn't force them to choose an animal they didn't want. Besides, it wouldn't be good for Buddy if the family had their hearts set on a puppy instead.

All the same, she wished that one of these families, one of these days, would just give Buddy a chance.

Didn't every pet deserve a chance?

Maybe next time, Buddy, Quinn thought.

The bookstore was just a few blocks away, but Quinn and her dad drove there anyway so that the young kittens wouldn't catch a chill.

"I'm going to drop you off right out front," Dad said. "I'll be back as soon as I find a parking space."

"Thanks, Dad," Quinn said gratefully. "Mrs. Alvarez said I didn't have to stay all day, but I kind of want to."

"We can stay as long as you want," Dad replied.

"Come on, kitties," Quinn said to the cats in the carrier. "Let's go find your family!"

After double-checking to make sure the carrier door was securely fastened, Quinn climbed out of the car, holding the carrier tightly in her arms. The bookstore was just a few doors down, but Quinn could already see a flurry of activity in the front window. James was putting the finishing touches on the display—and it was more incredible than Quinn had ever dreamed it could be!

An enormous, Victorian-style dollhouse filled the front window. It had four stories with real lights that glowed with soft warmth. As she looked closer, Quinn realized that each room was stocked with a different type of cat toy: There were catnip mice and feather toys and bouncy balls and a toy with a brass bell. Some of the rooms had soft velvet cushions— the perfect place for a sleepy kitten to take a nap!

Miniature icicles, glittering in the light, hung from the eaves of the dollhouse; a toy sleigh pulled by eight reindeer was perched on top of the roof. Above that was a banner that read 'TWAS THE NIGHT BEFORE CHRISTMAS; garlands of tiny twinkle lights made the scene even more festive.

And the dollhouse wasn't all. Outside of it was a large, pretend park with all kinds of kitten-sized equipment—swings, a slide, and a merry-go-round!

Best of all, though, was the beautiful sign hanging behind the display. It read:

This holiday season,
open your home.
Open your heart.
Paisley, Polka, and Dot
need a family.
Could it be *you*?

Quinn, beaming, knocked on the window to get James's attention. He turned around and waved.

"This is amazing!" Quinn yelled through the glass. "Incredible!"

"Come on in," James said, beckoning to her. "I'm almost done!"

Quinn hurried inside the door, where Juniper was placing trays of fresh-baked cookies on the counter. "Morning, Quinn!" she said brightly. "Want a cookie?

Technically, they're for Santa, but I don't think he'll mind sharing."

"Thanks!" Quinn replied. "Juniper—the display—it's *perfect*! I don't even know what to say."

"Glad you like it!" Juniper replied. "James and I were brainstorming, and we wanted, you know, a literary theme—so of course ''Twas the Night Before Christmas' came to mind right away. Can you get more adorable than kittens in a dollhouse?"

"I doubt it," Quinn replied.

Juniper's eyes twinkled. "So what do you think… are they ready to move in?"

"Let's do it!" Quinn said.

Juniper led Quinn across the store to the front window. "There's a little door here," she said, showing Quinn the small door that led to the display. "Want to go in?"

"Into the display?" Quinn asked in surprise.

"Sure! It's fun," Juniper replied. "Cramped but fun."

Quinn pushed the cat carrier through the small door, then climbed through herself.

"Hey, Quinn," James said. "What do you think? Any suggestions?"

Quinn shook her head. "It's perfect," she said. "And the kittens are going to *love* it!"

"I can't wait to see what they do," James said. "All right...now for the moment of truth...release the kittens!"

Quinn knelt down to open up the cat carrier. Paisley, Polka, and Dot were huddled together at the back. For a long moment, they just stared at her.

"Come on, kittties," Quinn said in her calmest, most soothing voice. "You can come out now!"

But they still didn't budge.

For the first time that day, Quinn started to worry. *What if they're too nervous to come out?* she wondered. *What if they're too scared to play like they do back at the shelter?*

"I have an idea," James said. He plucked one of the feather toys from the dollhouse and dangled it in front of the carrier door.

Dot cocked her head. She took a tentative step forward...then another one....

James moved the feather a little farther away....

Dot followed it....

Quinn, holding her breath, didn't move a muscle.

Just a few more steps and Dot would be out of the carrier. The tiny kitten hesitated. Her body was perfectly still. Only her eyes moved, ever so slightly, as she watched the feather toy twitch and tremble. Then—

Whoosh!

In a blur of fur, Dot bounded out of the carrier, with Polka chasing her tail. Quinn giggled as she scooped up the kittens and placed them in the dollhouse. Soon they were running up and down the stairs, chasing each other through the rooms and pausing only to play with the toys they discovered along the way.

When Paisley came out of the carrier, Quinn knew it was time to get out of the display so that the cats could be the stars of the show. James made a few adjustments to the webcam; then he and Quinn crawled through the little door again.

"How does it look?" James asked Juniper, who was staring at her phone.

Juniper glanced up with a grin. She held out her phone so James and Quinn could see the screen. "And we're streaming!" she announced.

"The kittens are live?" Quinn squealed.

Juniper nodded. "Hang on...gotta post the link...."

Quinn reached for her phone, too. She wanted to text it to everyone she knew—from Mrs. Alvarez and Ms. Ferrino to Annabelle and Eliza.

Just then, Dad walked into the bookstore. "You're attracting quite a crowd out there," he told Quinn. "The kittens are going to have a pretty big fan club when all's said and done. So what happens now?"

"Now...we wait," Quinn replied.

The bookstore was bustling with activity all day: A volunteer wearing a Santa suit posed for pictures with kids, while James and Juniper helped customers find the perfect book and managed to keep warm cookies, fresh from the little oven, on the counter all day. Quinn helped however she could—while keeping an eye on the kittens, too. She couldn't believe how many people were watching the video of them play on the bookstore website! Quinn had to believe that at least a few of them would be moved to adopt Paisley and her kittens.

After all, how could they resist?

Chapter 9

On Monday nights, the shelter was open late, which was good for Quinn since her dad often had a big deadline that kept him stuck in his office way past dinner. Mrs. Alvarez never minded if Quinn stayed until closing. She usually ordered a couple of pizzas for the staff, who were always happy to share with Quinn.

Quinn was sitting by the electric fireplace as she started painting an ornament with Paisley's face on it. She glanced at her list. After Paisley came ornaments for Polka and Dot, and then she wanted to make one of Snowdrop for Eliza's family, and of course one for Annabelle of her dog, Bumblebee. Quinn smiled as she remembered painting a brown version of Bumblebee on her very first ornament. So much had happened since then!

And then...after the last ornament for Annabelle...would Quinn be done? Orders continued trickling in, but the truth was that there were only four more days until Christmas. She had a feeling that demand for ornaments would dry up pretty suddenly once Christmas was over. And even though Quinn knew a part of her would miss the constant ornament painting, she was excited to start working on her sculpture make-up project over Christmas break.

Best of all, Quinn had almost enough money for her ticket to California! It had become a habit to check the flight costs on her phone every night before she went to bed. As soon as Annabelle knew about Quinn's big surprise, they could pick a date. Dad would book her ticket, and then it was only a matter of time before she and Annabelle would be together again! Quinn had never been to California before, but she could imagine it: sunshine and palm trees and swimming pools and flowers blooming everywhere, all year round. But she didn't need to use her imagination to know how incredible it would be to hang out with Annabelle once more!

"It's so quiet here tonight," Quinn said as she added some glittering yellow stars around Paisley's profile.

"Maybe because the weekend was so busy," Tommy said as he reached for another slice of pizza.

"Not only did we get *seven* applications for the kittens and their mama, we got applications for the puppies, too—all five of them!" added Mrs. Alvarez. "I really think the Twelve Pets of Christmas program has been a huge success—even if all twelve pets don't find homes before Christmas, our overall adoption rate has been through the roof."

"But it's not over yet," Quinn said. "There are still three more pets that need to find homes." She counted them off on her fingers. "Tops and Tippy and Buddy."

"Yes, that's right," Mrs. Alvarez said. "There's still four days. Anything's possible. But we should be realistic. For those dogs to be in new homes *before* Christmas, we'd need applications by tomorrow at the latest—and even then, it would be a stretch. We always knew that Tops and Tippy would be a challenging placement. It's hard to find a home for two dogs at once, and even harder when one of them is as big as Tops."

"But it's Christmas!" Quinn insisted. "It's the season of miracles. Anything can happen."

"And maybe it will," Mrs. Alvarez said, staring out at the parking lot as a car pulled in. Its headlights arced through the icy darkness. "Tommy—is that the couple who came in over the weekend?"

"I think so," her son replied as he peered out the window, too. "They were here for a couple of hours on Saturday afternoon. They were interested in a dog, right?"

Buddy! Quinn thought hopefully as her heart started pounding. Could this be his chance at last?

She put down her paintbrush as a man and a woman walked through the door.

"Hi there," Tommy said. "Good to see you again."

"Are you closing?" the woman asked. "We tried to get here right after work."

"It's fine," Mrs. Alvarez assured them. "How can we help you?"

The woman and man exchanged a gleeful smile.

"I can't believe we're doing this," he said, "but I think we'd like to adopt *two* dogs."

"The big one and the little one," his wife added. "We just couldn't stop thinking about them all weekend! I love that they're so inseparable."

"Kind of like us," her husband replied, reaching for her hand.

"We want to make sure they stay together—forever," the woman added. "Plus, they're so funny! Great big Tops and tiny Tippy."

"This is fantastic news!" said Mrs. Alvarez. "If you can just fill out these forms for me, I'll call your references first thing tomorrow morning."

"Can I spend some time with the dogs while Ted fills out the forms?" the woman asked.

"Sure," Quinn said. "I'll take you back to see them."

"I still can't believe we're doing this," the woman

confided in Quinn. "We've never had two dogs before—just one at a time. And after our last dog, Sandy, died, we were so heartbroken that we thought we might never have another pet."

Quinn smiled sympathetically. "It's so hard," she said. "We have a lot of clients who feel that way after they lose a pet. Mrs. Alvarez says that time heals, though."

"I agree with that," the woman said, nodding. "Even two months ago, we definitely weren't ready. But now—we really are."

Quinn opened the door to Tops and Tippy's pen. "It's more comfortable in the visiting room," Quinn told the woman. "I'll send your husband back when he finishes the application."

"Thank you!" the woman said.

Quinn didn't go straight back to the front desk, though. Instead, she stopped by Buddy's pen. "Hey, Buddy," she said.

Buddy was curled up in the corner again, staring at the wall, but his tail went *thump-thump-thump* when he heard Quinn's voice. Charlie had visited that afternoon, but he'd been gone for a few hours.

The change in Buddy was so dramatic, if Quinn hadn't seen it with her own eyes, she never would've believed it. When Charlie was there, Buddy was happy, joyful, filled with energy.

And when Charlie wasn't there? Buddy was quiet. Lonely. Sad. Quinn tried not to dwell on what Christmas would be like for Buddy if he wasn't adopted in the next couple of days. She knew that on Christmas Day, one of the workers would stop by to feed the animals and check on them—but otherwise, it would be a long and lonely day for Buddy. He wouldn't understand it was a holiday. He'd probably wait all day long for Charlie to come visit. Maybe he would even wonder where Quinn was. The thought made tears spring to her eyes—and made her even more determined to find a family for Buddy.

"Don't give up, Buddy," Quinn said. "I still have hope. There's still a chance!"

Chapter 10

On Christmas Eve morning, Quinn's eyes flew open just as the sun was starting to rise. Technically, there was no reason for her to be awake at the crack of dawn. She was on Christmas break—school had let out the day before—but who could sleep in on Christmas Eve? Not Quinn! Not when there were presents to wrap and cookies to bake and the last couple of ornaments to deliver. Plus, she wanted to stop by the pet store to buy Buddy a Christmas present—a new bone or maybe a squeaky toy. It was the least she could do, since it seemed she wouldn't be able to keep her promise after all.

Quinn quickly got dressed, choosing her favorite jeans and a cherry-red sweater. For fun, she decided to wear her Christmas earrings before she had to pack them away for another year. They were shaped like little bells, and they rang every time she moved her head.

"Morning, Quinn," her dad said when she came into the kitchen. "You look just like one of Santa's helpers."

"Merry Christmas Eve, Dad!" Quinn cried. "I couldn't sleep in today—even if I tried. Hey, can you give me a ride?"

"Sure," Dad replied. "Where do you need to go?"

"Downtown," she said. "I need to do a little shopping."

Dad made a funny face. "Shopping? On Christmas Eve?" he groaned. "Are you crazy?"

Quinn had to laugh. "I just have to buy one thing," she told him. "At the pet store. I want to get a present for Buddy."

"I take it he didn't get adopted?" Dad asked.

Quinn shook her head. "Not yet," she said. "Maybe it will happen after Christmas. Maybe

Buddy will have a very happy New Year instead of a merry Christmas."

Dad reached for his wallet. "Do you need any money for Buddy's present?"

"No, I can pay for it myself," Quinn said quickly. "I've saved all my ornament money and—"

Quinn's voice trailed off unexpectedly.

"And what?" Dad prompted her.

"I…" Quinn said.

Dad started to look concerned. "Are you okay?"

"I…hang on. I need to…check something," Quinn said. "Be right back!"

Quinn slid off her chair and hurried back to her room. Her heart was pounding in her chest, even as she tried not to get too excited—not yet, anyway. It was just an idea—a crazy, wild, unexpected, and unpredictable idea—but if it worked—and it just might work—

Quinn's hand was trembling as she reached for the little notebook where she'd been keeping track of the money she'd made from painting ornaments. It was true—she really had saved every penny that she'd earned. Dad had assured her that it would be

133

enough for an airplane ticket to California, with a little extra for spending money, too.

But would it—*could* it—also be enough to fund Buddy's adoption?

If the *only* reason why Ms. Ferrino and Charlie weren't able to adopt Buddy was money—couldn't Quinn help with that? It would mean no trip to California—at least, not during spring break—but Quinn didn't hesitate, not for a second.

She reached for a pen and started making a list:

* *Food*
* *Dog bed and toys*
* *Leash, collar, tags?*
* *Vet bills*

Quinn wasn't sure how much all of that would cost. But she knew how to find out.

A few hours later, Quinn rushed into the Marion Animal Shelter.

"Merry, merry!" Mrs. Alvarez called from the

front desk. "You just missed Charlie. He and his mother stopped by to give Buddy a bone."

"Mrs. Alvarez," Quinn said in a rush, "I had an idea."

Something about Quinn's voice made Mrs. Alvarez put down her pen. "I'm listening."

"I want to sponsor Buddy's adoption," Quinn announced. She placed her notebook on Mrs. Alvarez's desk and continued speaking in a rush. "I spent all morning trying to figure out how much it costs to have a dog for a year. I priced out a year's worth of food and figured maybe two visits to the vet? I know Buddy is already up to date on all his shots. And I looked up the costs for registering your dog with the county, and getting him new tags with the Ferrinos' address printed on them, and I have enough. I have enough money saved up for all of it."

"Whoa, whoa, whoa," Mrs. Alvarez said, holding up her hand. "Slow down. *You* want to adopt Buddy?"

Quinn shook her head. "No, not me," she explained. "I want to pay for the Ferrinos to adopt him. Don't you see? It's perfect! Buddy and Charlie get to be together—and Buddy gets to go home for Christmas!"

"But how did—"

"My ornament money," Quinn answered before Mrs. Alvarez could finish her question. "I was going to buy a plane ticket to visit Annabelle...but making sure Buddy has a home is more important. I can save up more money. Maybe I can visit Annabelle next summer instead."

Mrs. Alvarez's smile was quivering, like she was feeling something much more than simple happiness.

"Will it work?" Quinn asked, an edge of nervousness in her voice. "Do my figures make sense?"

Mrs. Alvarez glanced at Quinn's notebook. The moments before she answered felt like an eternity to Quinn. At last, Mrs. Alvarez looked up.

"You worked hard to earn that money, Quinn," she said. "Are you sure you want to do this?"

"Positive," Quinn replied. "I've never been this sure about anything. Will it work? Did I forget anything?"

"It looks good to me," Mrs. Alvarez finally said.

"I mean, we can't predict the future. But, to answer your question, yes—the amount of money you've saved for Buddy's care should last at least a year."

Quinn started to cheer, but Mrs. Alvarez stopped her. "What about the second year, though?" she asked. "Remember, Ms. Ferrino won't be done with nursing school for two more years."

"More ornaments," Quinn said right away. "I'll advertise next fall. I'm sure I'll be able to get more orders. Maybe I can hang a sign here—so everyone who adopts a pet will be able to order one. And I was also thinking I might start doing pet portraits. Something you could frame and hang on the wall...and something people would want to buy all year."

"That's a great idea," Mrs. Alvarez said. "I think you'd have a lot of customers, young lady."

"So can we do it?" Quinn asked, her voice high and hopeful. "Can we bring Buddy to the Ferrinos' house *today*?"

"Maybe," Mrs. Alvarez said. "But I have to talk to Ms. Ferrino first."

"But then she'll know about the surprise," Quinn said.

"We have to get her permission," Mrs. Alvarez said. "It would be against all our regulations to send a dog to someone's house when they weren't expecting it."

Quinn didn't like it, but she had to admit that Mrs. Alvarez made a good point. "Can it at least be a surprise for Charlie?" she asked.

"That's up to his mother," Mrs. Alvarez said as she reached for the phone. "I'll call her right now. Do you want to spend some time with Buddy while I'm on the phone?"

From the way Mrs. Alvarez said it, Quinn could tell it wasn't a question. For whatever reason, Mrs. Alvarez didn't want Quinn to hear her side of the conversation. Quinn was on her way to the dog wing when she heard Mrs. Alvarez say, "Hello, is this Olivia? This is Anita Alvarez calling from Marion Animal Shelter."

Quinn slipped into Buddy's pen. He looked up and his tail went *thump-thump-thump*.

She sat next to Buddy and started to pet his

back. "This could be it, Buddy," she whispered. Her thoughts were pounding like her heartbeat: *I hope, I hope, I hope.*

The minutes ticked away while Quinn waited for Mrs. Alvarez to finish her conversation. Ms. Ferrino *had* to say yes! This was it: the Christmas miracle that Quinn—and Buddy—had been waiting for.

At last, Quinn heard footsteps. Buddy heard them, too. They jumped up at the same time as Mrs. Alvarez and Tommy appeared in the hallway.

"Well?" Quinn asked. "What did she say?"

"She said...*yes!*" Mrs. Alvarez exclaimed as her face broke into a beaming smile.

"Yes!" Quinn shrieked. "Yes, yes, yes, *yes!*"

Then Quinn was hugging Buddy and Buddy was barking and Tommy and Mrs. Alvarez were laughing, and Quinn was so happy that she wanted to cry and laugh and sing all at the same time.

"You're going home, Buddy!" Quinn cried. "Home to your new family! Home to Charlie!"

Buddy tilted his head as he looked at her, puzzled. She knew he didn't understand—how could he? But he'd heard Charlie's name, and he knew who

Charlie was, and soon they'd be together all the time. Quinn's heart was so filled with happiness it felt like it could burst.

"Can we take him right now?" Quinn asked.

Mrs. Alvarez glanced at her watch. "Soon," she said. "We've got to get supplies for him from the pet store."

"I'll go," Tommy volunteered.

"Here," Quinn told him, pressing an envelope of money into his hands. "I left my list on the front counter."

"Be back as soon as I can," Tommy promised.

Mrs. Alvarez turned to Quinn. "Okay!" she said. "Let's get Buddy ready to go."

"Ready to go?" Quinn repeated. "What do you mean?"

"Bath, brushing, clip his nails," Mrs. Alvarez replied. "The works!"

"I get it!" Quinn giggled. "A doggy makeover!"

"Exactly," Mrs. Alvarez said. "Follow me!"

Mrs. Alvarez led Quinn and Buddy to the grooming room. The gleaming white tile room had a few different grooming stations, complete with sprayers attached to rubber hoses.

"I've never helped with dog grooming before," Quinn said.

"Well, let me get you the most important tool you'll need," Mrs. Alvarez said as she disappeared into the storage room. Quinn wondered what it would be. The nail clippers? A brush? Special dog shampoo?

But when Mrs. Alvarez returned, she wasn't carrying any of those. Instead, her arms were filled with raincoats!

"I learned the hard way," Mrs. Alvarez told Quinn as she handed her one of the raincoats. "Wet dogs like to shake—and it feels just like being in a rainstorm!"

Quinn pulled on the raincoat and zipped it up. It was too big for her, but she figured that would just give her extra protection from the doggy downpour. "How do I look?" Quinn joked. "I feel runway ready—not that Buddy and I should hit the runway again anytime soon!"

Mrs. Alvarez laughed. Then she reached for a bottle of lavender-scented dog shampoo. "Ready, Buddy?" she asked. "We're going to get you all cleaned up for Christmas!"

Mrs. Alvarez showed Quinn all her best dog grooming tricks—how to clip Buddy's nails so that they were neat and even (but not too short); how to wash his coat without getting any soap in his eyes; and how to brush his fur until his coat gleamed. Buddy, who'd spent so many lonesome days living in the shelter, loved every moment of the special attention. The look on his face was pure bliss.

By the time Quinn and Mrs. Alvarez finished, Tommy had returned from the pet store. "You would not believe the crowds," he said as he dropped several huge bags on the floor. "Whoa!"

"That bad?" Mrs. Alvarez asked.

"Worse," Tommy said. "Looks like everybody in Marion had to make a few last-minute purchases today. But never fear, I got everything on your list, Quinn."

Tommy started rummaging in one of the bags.

"And I even got something that wasn't on your list!" he announced happily, holding up a doggy-sized Santa hat. "Don't worry—I bought it with my own money," he quickly added. "You worked way too hard on those ornaments for me to waste your money on something this silly."

Quinn wasn't worried, though—she was cracking up! She took the hat from Tommy and perched it on Buddy's head. He looked up at them, blinking, as his pink tongue lolled out of his mouth.

Thump-thump-thump!

"There goes Buddy's tail," Mrs. Alvarez said. "I think that's his seal of approval!"

"He looks great," Quinn said happily.

"Oh!" Tommy exclaimed. "I almost forgot!"

He rummaged around in the shopping bag one more time and pulled out a length of red velvet ribbon. "How about a bow around Buddy's neck?" he suggested.

"Absolutely," Quinn replied. She knelt down to tie the ribbon in a big, floppy bow—and was rewarded with a kiss from Buddy when he licked her cheek.

"Buddy, you've never looked more festive," Mrs. Alvarez declared. Then she reached into her pocket, pulled out her keys, and jingled them in the air. "What do you think, Quinn? Ready to go?"

"Absolutely," Quinn said. "We've been ready for a while now—haven't we, Buddy?"

Thump-thump-thump!

Chapter 11

Tommy offered to stay behind at the shelter to feed the other animals while Mrs. Alvarez and Quinn took Buddy to Charlie's house. It was late afternoon, and the sun had just started to set. Quinn knew that the days would get longer and lighter soon, now that they'd passed the winter solstice. But for now, it was still dark well before dinnertime.

Buddy knew that this was no ordinary day. Quinn held tightly to his leash as they walked through the parking lot to Mrs. Alvarez's car. There was definitely an extra spring in Buddy's step; he was almost prancing, sniffing eagerly at the air and looking in every direction.

"Ready for a ride?" Quinn asked as she opened the car door for Buddy. She slid in after him, buckled her seat belt, and put her arm reassuringly on Buddy's back. She could hardly believe that the moment was here at last: Buddy's adoption! After all those weeks of wondering and worrying, things were happening faster than Quinn had ever expected. She couldn't imagine what the shelter would be like without Buddy there to greet her every day. She could already tell she was going to miss him.

Ms. Ferrino and Charlie lived only a few blocks from the shelter. *Maybe*, Quinn thought, *they'll let me come visit Buddy once in a while*. Mrs. Alvarez pulled up in front of a small brick house. Quinn grinned when she saw the fence around the perimeter of the yard. It was the perfect yard for a dog; Quinn could just picture Buddy and Charlie playing Frisbee in the springtime...splashing in a wading pool in the summer...and jumping in leaf piles all fall.

It was going to be the life Buddy had always deserved.

"Here we are," Mrs. Alvarez said.

"Okay, Buddy," Quinn said, with a strange feeling of finality. "This is it! Ready to see your new home...and your favorite boy?"

Thump-thump-thump!

Quinn wrapped Buddy's leash around her hand, then opened the car door. She could see a Christmas tree gleaming with lights in the front window; there was a festive wreath on the door.

Buddy trotted along next to Quinn as they approached the front door. On the doorstep, she paused to straighten Buddy's Santa hat and adjust his bow. Then, impulsively, she reached down to give him one more giant hug.

"You're the best dog," she whispered near his ear. "Merry Christmas, Buddy."

Then Quinn reached out and pressed the doorbell with her gloved finger.

Ding-dong!

Quinn's heart was pounding so much that she

thought it might drown out the thumping of Buddy's tail.

"Mom! Somebody's here!" Charlie's voice was muffled by the door.

Quinn squeezed Buddy's leash in anticipation. This was it—this was the moment—

The door began to open, spilling warmth and light onto the doorstep. Charlie was standing there, with Ms. Ferrino behind him. Already her eyes were brimming with happy tears. But it was Charlie's face—and his wide, wondering eyes—that captured Quinn's full attention.

"Merry Christmas!" Quinn cried. She held out the leash to Charlie.

Charlie still didn't quite comprehend what was happening. It was too impossible to believe. He looked from Buddy to Quinn to his mom and back to Quinn.

"Buddy—" he began, unsure.

"Belongs to you," Quinn said. "He's your dog now. Forever and ever."

"But—" Charlie said. He glanced back at his mom, still unsure.

Ms. Ferrino kissed the top of his head and said, "Merry Christmas!"

And *that* was when Charlie really and truly understood. He lunged toward Buddy; at the same time, Buddy leaped up and put his paws on Charlie's shoulders. As Charlie staggered backward, Ms. Ferrino caught him, and then the three of them tumbled onto the floor, a noisy, happy mix of laughter and barking and Buddy's tail—always!—going *thump-thump-thump*.

Their joy was overwhelming. It was infectious. It was as warm and wonderful as the sun shining after a cold rain, and Quinn was inexpressibly grateful for the opportunity to stand on the front step and bask in it.

I'll slip away now, she thought, taking a quiet step backward. She didn't want to intrude on their special Christmas surprise. But before she could, Charlie looked over. He scrambled to his feet and gave Quinn a sudden, fierce hug.

"Thank you," he said. "Thank you for bringing Buddy to me."

Quinn smiled down at him. "Thank you for being Buddy's best friend," she replied.

Then Charlie turned back to Buddy. "Come on,

Buddy! You've gotta see my room!" he said. "You can sleep on my bed. My sheets are cool; they have trains and trucks."

"How can I thank you, Quinn?" Ms. Ferrino asked. "You've given Charlie the greatest Christmas present ever. I'll never be able to tell you how grateful I am."

"No," Quinn said quickly. "Thank *you* for adopting Buddy. I wanted him to have a home more than anything in the world." And as she said the words, Quinn realized how true they were.

"I *promise* I'll pay you back," Ms. Ferrino told her. "Every penny, just as soon as I've finished school."

But Quinn shook her head vehemently. "I wouldn't accept it. Being here—seeing this—it's payment enough."

Mrs. Alvarez joined them then, carrying a large bag from the pet store. "Oof," she said as she lowered it to the ground. "I don't know how Santa does it!"

Everyone laughed as Ms. Ferrino and Quinn helped Mrs. Alvarez finish unloading her car. It seemed like Tommy had bought out the entire pet store!

"Please come in," Ms. Ferrino said. "Would you like some cocoa and cookies?"

Mrs. Alvarez glanced at her watch. "I wish we could," she said. "But Tommy's waiting for me back at the shelter—and I want to drive Quinn home—"

"Of course—it's Christmas Eve," Ms. Ferrino replied. "You've got to get back to your own families. But maybe another time."

"*Definitely* another time," Quinn promised. "Merry Christmas, Ms. Ferrino!"

"Merry Christmas!" Ms. Ferrino called as Quinn and Mrs. Alvarez went back to the car.

Quinn was unusually quiet as Mrs. Alvarez drove her home. She stared out the car window at the night sky as the stars began to appear. Was it her imagination, or was one of them shining more brightly than the others? The longer Quinn looked, the more she believed that it was. And why shouldn't it be? It was Christmas Eve, after all. And Quinn knew better than anyone that *anything* could happen at Christmastime. Quinn had been longing for a Christmas miracle—but what she hadn't realized was that *she* had the power to make one happen.

"Merry Christmas," Quinn told Mrs. Alvarez when they arrived. "Thank you for—for everything."

"No, Quinn," Mrs. Alvarez replied. "Thank *you*."

Quinn climbed out of the car and looked up. That star really *was* shining brighter than the others—which didn't surprise Quinn one bit.

Chapter 12

"Merry Christmas, Dad!" Quinn shrieked as she bounded into her dad's bedroom. "Wake up! It's Christmas!"

Dad groaned a little as he pulled the pillow over his head. "Tell me it's not still dark outside," he said.

"Uh...let me check," Quinn replied as she dashed over to the window. "No, it's not dark. I mean, not really dark. I mean, it's not pitch black.... I *think* the sun's started to rise...or it's about to, anyway...."

Dad laughed as he pulled the pillow off his face. "I'm just kidding. Merry Christmas, sweetheart! I'm just going to get some Christmas coffee and then we can open Christmas presents."

"Presents!" Quinn shrieked gleefully.

A few minutes later, Quinn and her dad were sitting by the tree next to a small stack of presents. Quinn had a new skirt from her aunt and a stack of books from her grandparents. Then Dad passed her a large red box.

"I hope this is right," he said. "Let's just say I've never bought anything like it before."

Quinn's curiosity was piqued. She untied the ribbon slowly, savoring the anticipation of the moment. Then she lifted the lid…and looked down at a beautiful pair of brand-new ice skates with gleaming silver blades.

"Ice skates?" she cried. "Dad! This is incredible! Now I can go ice-skating with Eliza whenever I want!"

"You like them?" Dad asked, beaming.

"I *love* them! And I'm totally surprised!" Quinn replied. "How did you know about ice skates?"

"I heard you and Eliza talking about skating when she was hanging out here after school," he explained. "You two seem to get along so well—and I thought you might want to go skating with her sometime. I'm glad you've made a new friend, Quinn. I know it wasn't easy when Annabelle moved away."

"It wasn't," Quinn admitted. "And it still isn't... but it's getting better."

Then Quinn glanced around the tree. "I guess nothing came from Annabelle," she replied. "She told me she had a very special present, but I couldn't have it until Christmas Day."

Dad shrugged. "I only see one present left," he replied.

"That's for *you*," Quinn said. She gave Dad the box. Inside was the most special ornament of all, painted with their cat, Piper. Quinn had never felt more proud than when Dad hung it high on the tree.

After breakfast, Quinn glanced at the clock and sighed.

"What's wrong?" Dad asked.

"I want to call Annabelle, but it's three hours earlier there," she said. "I probably have to wait until afternoon, but that's, like, *hours* away."

"You can help me in the kitchen," Dad replied. "Let's get started cooking Christmas dinner."

"Okay," Quinn replied. "I'm going to make some cocoa first." When Quinn opened the fridge, she gasped. "Dad! There's so much food in here! The fridge is stuffed!"

"Well, you know," he began, "it *is* for Christmas dinner."

"Is that a whole *turkey*?" she exclaimed. "How are we going to eat all this food, Dad? It's way too much."

"I'm sure we'll think of something," he replied. He was leaning into the pantry to get something, so Quinn couldn't quite tell for sure—but it definitely sounded like he was laughing.

Just then, the doorbell rang. Quinn's shoulders straightened. "Dad?" she asked.

"Why don't you get the door?" Dad replied as he rummaged through the pantry. "I *know* there's cocoa powder in here somewhere...."

Quinn shrugged as she put the milk back in the fridge. She walked over to the front door, opened it...

And saw Annabelle and her parents standing on the doorstep!

Quinn was so surprised she couldn't say a word.

She must've made a funny face, though—her eyes all big and her mouth opened wide—because the Forresters burst into laughter.

"Surprise!" Annabelle shrieked as she flew forward to give Quinn a hug. "Merry Christmas!"

"You—you're—you're here!" Quinn cried, recovering from her shock. "But—I don't understand—*how*?"

Annabelle's eyes were twinkling. "I told you that your present was a *big* surprise!" she replied. "Oh, man! I didn't think I'd be able to keep the secret, but somehow I did!"

"We had to come back to Marion to finalize the sale of our house," Mrs. Forrester explained to Quinn. "It was Annabelle's idea to surprise you."

"We'll be here for four whole days!" Annabelle exclaimed. "And your dad already said I could sleep over—"

"Dad?" Quinn repeated. "Dad knew?" She remembered, suddenly, the fridge packed with food and turned around to see Dad standing behind her, grinning. "Dad! You knew!"

"Once I found out, I *had* to invite the Forresters for Christmas dinner," he replied. "Come in, come in! We've got coffee and tea—and Quinn was just about to make some cocoa—"

As Annabelle's parents followed Dad to the kitchen, Quinn shook her head in complete amazement. "I still can't believe you're here. I—this isn't the present I thought I'd give you today, but... Merry Christmas."

And she gave Annabelle the ornament she'd made.

"Quinn! It looks just like Bumblebee!" she exclaimed. "I can't believe you made one of your famous ornaments for me. Wow!"

"It's not much of a present," Quinn replied. "Your Christmas present was supposed to be a *much* bigger deal. I'd been saving all my ornament money so that I could come visit you, but..."

Annabelle's eyes got wider and wider as Quinn told her all about Buddy's Christmas Eve–miracle adoption. Then she impulsively reached out to give Quinn another hug.

"Of course you had to sponsor Buddy's adoption," Annabelle said right away. "I would've been *so mad* if you didn't!"

Quinn burst out laughing. "But how would you have known?"

"Because of my best friend super-psychic powers, of course," Annabelle declared. "You think moving to a new state weakened those? No way."

"I have a new plan to earn enough money for a plane ticket," Quinn said. "Hopefully I can visit you during the summer."

"That would be awesome," Annabelle replied. "I can't wait!"

"Girls!" Mrs. Forrester called. "Cocoa's ready."

Annabelle glanced at Quinn. "Mini marshmallows?" she asked.

"Whipped cream?" Quinn replied.

Then the best friends exchanged a smile and said the same thing, at the same time. "Both!" They giggled as they hurried to the kitchen.

Christmas joy filled Quinn's heart—especially when she thought about the Twelve Pets of Christmas, who were all waking up in their new homes. Quinn had a funny feeling that the pets—and their families—were as happy as she was. And that made it the best Christmas ever!

Not finished celebrating the season yet? Here's a sneak peek at another book in the series:

Celebrate the Season

Secret Snowflake

Taylor Garland

Secret Snowflake

"It's *snowing*!"

Those two words were guaranteed to get Riley Archer out of bed, no matter how early it was. Riley's eyes flew open as she fumbled for her phone on the bedside table, then squinted at the screen. It was only 6:12—her alarm wasn't supposed to go off for another eighteen minutes—but Riley didn't mind the earlier-than-usual wake up. Based on how loudly her little brother, Theo, was shouting about the snow, it sounded like today might be a snow day. If that was the case, Riley wanted to know about it!

Riley scrambled out of bed in such a rush that

she forgot to grab her glasses. She'd been wearing glasses for a month, but she still wasn't quite used to them. Across the room, Riley yanked open the curtains and saw...nothing out of the ordinary. There was the deserted gray sidewalk; the stubby brown grass; and the empty black streets, which were etched with odd patterns where the salt trucks had brined the roads overnight in anticipation of a storm. It was early enough that the streetlights were still on, casting a weak yellow glow as the sky gradually began to lighten.

"What snow?" Riley mumbled to herself. But it wasn't like Theo to make up a story—or get so excited about nothing. She reached for her glasses and took another look.

Sure enough, in the warm glow of the streetlights, Riley could see it: little flurries drifting down from the leaden sky. She had to grin. Theo got excited so easily. Yes, technically it was snowing. But unless those faint flurries suddenly swirled into a blizzard, there was no way school would be canceled today. There wouldn't even be a late start.

And—to be completely and totally honest—that

was okay with Riley. After all, it wasn't just any ordinary school day. It was the day Riley had been waiting for since September: the kickoff to Secret Snowflake! Ever since Riley had learned about Secret Snowflake on the first day of seventh grade, she'd been looking forward to it. Secret Snowflake was just one of the things that made Mrs. Darlington, Riley's homeroom and language arts teacher, so awesome. She was really into all kinds of different, creative assignments (Mrs. D. called them "alternative learning opportunities," whatever that meant). To Riley, the unusual projects were interesting, exciting, and sometimes even fun—and they made her really look forward to school.

Take Secret Snowflake, for example. In a few hours, the students in Mrs. Darlington's class would pick names and, for the next two weeks, exchange small, secret gifts every day. Sure, there was some schoolwork involved—Riley was supposed to keep a daily journal about her Secret Snowflake experience and write an essay at the end of the project—but for the most part, Riley already knew that Secret Snowflake was going to be incredibly fun!

Might as well get ready for school, Riley thought. She'd already planned her entire outfit, from her ice-blue sweater to her favorite pair of boots. As a finishing touch, Riley decided to wear her dangling snowflake earrings, too.

By the time Riley got downstairs, Theo was already eating a stack of pancakes at the kitchen table. "Did you see?" he asked excitedly. "It's snowing! Maybe we won't have to go to school today!"

Riley paused to ruffle up Theo's blond hair, grinning as he ducked away from her. "Flurries," she corrected him. "They're not going to cancel classes for a little bit of snow. But, who knows—maybe school will close early if it picks up!"

Theo looked disappointed—but only for a moment. "It's still *snow*, Riley," he insisted. "That's better than nothing! And maybe it will get really heavy this afternoon and we can go sledding later."

"Sure," Riley said with a laugh. "Anything's possible."

After breakfast, Riley peeked into her backpack to make sure she had everything. Her binder, her books, her lunch—check, check, and check. Most important, though, Riley had remembered to pack her personalized snowflake, the very first part of the Secret Snowflake assignment. At the start of the week, Mrs. Darlington had given each student a plain snowflake made out of heavy cardstock and told them to decorate it so that it reflected their personalities. It was more challenging than it sounded, but Riley had really enjoyed the assignment. She had placed her school picture in the center of the snowflake and used each branch to highlight a different interest—music notes, a drawing of a rabbit, a chocolate cupcake, and a photo of her family. Then she'd filled in all the blank spaces with sparkly blue glitter. By the time she'd finished, Riley was really proud of her snowflake. Not only was it pretty enough that she planned to hang it in her room when she got to take it home, but it really did reflect her personality—and all the things that mattered most to her.

"Bye, Mom! Bye, Dad! Bye, Theo!" Riley called as she wrapped her scarf around her neck. "See you after school!"

Then she paused in the doorway. Was it snowing harder already? "Or maybe sooner!" Riley added.

※ ※ ※

By the time Riley got to homeroom, she could tell she wasn't the only one excited about Secret Snowflake. Some of the kids were trying to act cool, like they didn't really care, but almost everybody else was chatting excitedly about it. Riley's best friend, Sophia, practically pounced on her the moment she walked through the door.

"Can you believe? Secret Snowflake? Is finally here?" Sophia asked breathlessly. Her excitement made it sound like she was asking a bunch of rapid-fire questions.

"I know!" Riley exclaimed. "And there are only two more weeks until Christmas break, too!"

"Come on! Let's hang up our snowflakes!" Sophia said as she pulled Riley across the room.

Together, the two girls hung their snowflakes on the window. The ledge under the window was crowded with boxes that would hold the Secret Snowflake presents.

"I wonder who will pick our names," Sophia said. "Tell the truth. Is there anybody you're hoping for?"

Riley shrugged. "Not really," she said, trying to sound casual. "I'd be happy with anybody."

Riley watched her friend closely to see if Sophia had noticed that Riley was keeping something from her. Because the truth was that Riley *did* hope, in her secret-most heart, that she would pick Marcus Anderson...or that Marcus would pick her. She'd had a crush on Marcus for almost two years now, and Secret Snowflake seemed like it would be the perfect chance to show him how she really felt.

Luckily, Sophia's thoughts had already flitted off to another topic. "Do you think it will be hard? To come up with ten different presents?" she said. "I mean, it would be easy if I pick your name. I know you so well! But what if I pick somebody who I don't know that well? What then?"

"That's what the snowflakes are for, I guess—to give a few hints," Riley replied. "Plus, I think that's supposed to be part of the challenge. Getting to know your person a little better and all that."

Just then, Marcus entered the room, with Mrs. Darlington right behind him. "Good morning, class," Mrs. Darlington announced. "If you haven't already hung your snowflake on the window, please do so now. Then go ahead and take your seats."

Riley hurried across the room to her desk, tucking her hair behind her ears as she snuck a glance at Marcus. He was standing by the window, goofing with Austin as the boys hung up their snowflakes. She didn't want Marcus to catch her staring...but if he happened to glance her way at the same time, well, that would be pretty incredible....

As the bell rang, Mrs. Darlington placed a small silver box on her desk. "And now, the moment we've all been waiting for," she announced with a big smile. "One by one, I'll call you to come pick a name for your Secret Snowflake. Remember, once you pull a name, you're sworn to secrecy! We'll go in alphabetical order. Marcus Anderson."

Riley watched as Marcus got up from the seat in front of her, ambled across the classroom, and pulled a slip of paper out of the box. He read it, smiled, and slipped it into his pocket. Then he looked right at Riley—and smiled again!

Why did he do that? Had Marcus picked her name? Was he giving her a *sign*?

Riley's heart was pounding with such anticipation that she almost didn't hear Mrs. Darlington call her name.

"Riley Archer," Mrs. Darlington repeated. "Riley?"

The class started to giggle.

Riley didn't care, though. Marcus Anderson had *smiled* at her! She hurried up to the front of the room, thrust her hand into the box, and shut her eyes. Her fingers closed around a scrap of paper and, with her heart still pounding, Riley pulled it out.

Who would be her Secret Snowflake?

Riley was about to find out!